The Mustard Seed Kids

Praying for Rainbows

INSPIRED BY THE FAMILY OF JACKIE CARPENTER

MICHAEL MCCLENDON

ISBN: 978-1-4834-9653-5 (sc)
ISBN: 978-1-4834-9652-8 (hc)
ISBN: 978-1-4834-9654-2 (e)

Library of Congress Control Number: 2019900566

Lulu Publishing Services rev. date: 01/23/2019

Contents

Acknowledgments

Michael McClendon

My undying gratitude to my fuzzy and four-
legged family, for unconditional love.

Thank you to the amazing Connie Edwards, whose spirit
and expertise elevated every page of this novel.

I am grateful for the gift of Jackie Carpenter and her
loving family. Jackie has made an everlasting impression
on my life, and I am a better person because of her.

My thanks to every person who has continued
to love me, even when I didn't like me.

And in a very real and humble manner, I thank God for
The Words...and for allowing me to write them down.

Acknowledgments

Jackie Carpenter

My gratitude to Michael McClendon for having the
God given ability and talent to take my story and bring
it to life in a way that will change lives forever.

Thank you to my husband Larry Carpenter
for continuous love & support.

My two sons and daughters-in-law for their love
& encouragement and unwavering faith (Jim and
Jennifer Veitch/Jason and Stephanie Veitch).

Most of all to my four grandchildren: JJ, Hannah, Anna
Grace, and Patience for setting an example to all of us
regarding childlike FAITH thru the power of Psalm 91.

Introduction

In February of 2008, a tragedy occurred just a few miles from my Georgia home. Having recently sworn off local news, I heard nothing of it. I was too busy balancing several careers and taking care of personal crises, bills, work...you know, life.

I lived in a rural area; in a hundred-year-old house on seven wooded acres. I loved the trees and birds, the deer and the solitude. Perfect for writing and thinking and healing. But suddenly I had a problem. Copper thieves were cutting phone lines on a regular basis. It was so easy for these thieves to pull off onto my road, where they were hidden by woods and darkness, put a man at each end of the line, snip; into the truck bed, and then disappear onto the main road before anyone could think about catching them. At least once a week, my security system would begin to screech as lines were cut. Once repaired, they were often cut again within hours. This went on for a year. No home security system, no internet, no phone. It was madness. My work suffered. My sleep suffered. My peace of mind was shot. Until it happens to you, you cannot imagine the frustration.

In 2011, I was approached about writing a screenplay based on a real-life trial. I was given transcripts, recordings, and two books to research the event. What I found was jaw-dropping.

At the same time I was begging for help with the cut lines, another man living just down the road was dealing with something similar. He was a builder and his houses were being stripped of copper. They had stripped his houses seventeen times. And he was responsible for replacing it all out of his own pocket. As soon as he paid to replace it, they would strip them again. And as with my situation, he got no help. This seemed to be a crime that had no consequences. And it was fast and easy to execute, and safely get away. This man tried everything he could think of. Finally a police officer gave him some advice. And that's where things went terribly wrong.

Looking back, I realize the same thieves hitting my house had also been hitting the property of the man I was to write about, and at the very same time. Some things are just meant to be.

At the end of two years, I had not only written, but had cast and directed the film *STAND YOUR GROUND*. It was an uphill battle all the way, as it often is with Indie films. But the impact that this little film, and the novelization of the film, has had on so many people, makes it more than worthwhile.

The film *STAND YOUR GROUND*, and the book version, *A MOUNTAIN TOO HIGH*, focused on the struggle of the adults in this man's family. But I began to wonder how these events impacted the children. And so begins our story.

When I was just a little kid, something bad happened to my daddy. I wanted it to go away. Now I understand that it will never go away. And it didn't happen only to my daddy. It happened to all of us. And to people we didn't even know. And it's still happening.

My grandmother says that if we are still and listen very patiently, we can hear the voice of God. This is the story of my daddy and our family and how we learned to listen.

Chapter One

Over the River and into the Woods

———◇———

L ate February in Georgia can be tricky. Winter no longer has a full stranglehold on the south, but warm days are fleeting and not to be trusted. On this midday in 2008, spring had announced its impending arrival with a pale hint of green on the trees; a glowing frog-belly hue that would burst into white and pink when the dogwoods felt safe and warm. Jim Veitch looked out the bedroom window as he stuffed a work shirt into his Saturday pants. The back yard had lost its flatness and showed little waves and ripples that would soon need mowing. For a good six months his Saturdays would be filled with yard work, but he welcomed it. His best Sunday sermons came to him as he watched his push mower devour the lawn, leaving smooth, flat pathways in its wake. But no mowing today. Jim was going to help his little brother Jason pick up a Bobcat and start clearing acres of kudzu before it bloomed and created an impenetrable jungle. With Jason building

1

new houses and Jim preaching the gospel, the times the brothers found to do things together were few. This would be a good day.

In Jim's daughters' bedroom, nine-year-old Hannah Veitch was doggedly attempting to loop a belt onto the playsuit of her youngest sister, Patience. Pay-Pay was singing her favorite song, which consisted of only one line sung to an ever-improvised tune, and this day she was insisting on adding her own choreography. Belt loop almost done. Nope, it slipped out again.

Jennifer stuck her head into her daughters' bedroom and spoke over the song. "Patience, if you stand still, we can hear your song so much better."

And the dancing was done. Just as quickly, Hannah mouthed "thank you" to her mom and slipped the yellow belt through the tiny loops in the dotted Swiss outfit. But Pay-Pay's song was reprised. "Oh, the monkeys have no tails, Oh! the monkeys have no tails, Oh! the monkeys have no tails..."

"That's a pretty song, baby; what's it about?"

"Turtles and fwogs and —"

"Monkeys?"

"No, Mama! Turtles and fwogs and lizards! Ohhhhhhhhh! the monkeys have no tails..."

Most folks just come into a room. And then there are those who make an entrance. And so it was with the middle sister, seven-year-old Anna Grace. Her Sunday-best dress was complemented by a woman's Easter hat and an adult-size purse. Jennifer, attempting to organize the chaos on the girls' white and gold dresser, caught a glimpse of her daughter's ensemble in the mirror, and announced, "Anna Grace, you are not wearing a hat and purse to the zoo."

With a cry of despair, Anna Grace made an exit even more dramatic than her entrance. Her voice pled from beyond the doorway. "Then can I wear —"

"No."

"Then what if I just —"

"No, ma'am."

After a moment, Anna Grace re-entered the room grandly. She had doffed the hat, but was wearing a bejeweled pair of adult sunglasses.

Jennifer used the mommy eyes in the back of her head and didn't even look up as she commanded, "No."

"But Gommi says —"

"Anna Grace, when you get to be your grandmother's age, you can wear sunglasses and high heels and carry a purse to the zoo. Today you're wearing your green jumpsuit and tennis shoes."

"Mom, you have no fashion sense!"

"I don't have *time* for fashion sense!"

"I'll be a social outcast!" And Anna Grace disappeared with a grand flourish.

"Be a social outcast in a jumpsuit!"

Family hound Thumper entered the room, wearing the Easter hat. Thumper was resigned to wearing whatever Anna Grace fancied, and seemed to be content with the fact that, for the time being, he only wore a hat. With a sigh, he collapsed on Jennifer's feet. Jennifer tugged at her hair with a plastic doll brush and glimpsed Jim as he passed by the girls' room. "Jim, tell your brother —"

"Jason's not here yet."

"I know, but tell him when he gets here..."

"That...?"

"That I got some jars of homemade chili sauce for him and Stephanie!"

Hannah turned to her mom. "And for JJ, too."

Jennifer pulled the brush from her hair and turned to Hannah. "JJ doesn't eat chili sauce."

"Because of boogers," added Patience.

Jim stepped into the room. "What?"

Patience replied with solemn certainty, "JJ won't eat chili sauce, because it's made with boogers."

Hannah turned up her nose. "He did not say that!"

Unruffled, Patience responded, "Well somebody said something about boogers."

Anna Grace slipped nonchalantly past her dad and back into the bedroom. She was wearing, as Jennifer ordered, her green jumpsuit and tennis shoes. She also sported a black hat with a veil, and her tennies were stuffed into Jennifer's black heels. In a cultured whisper, she chided Patience, "Don't say boogers."

"Well then, what do I say instead?"

Anna Grace turned to Jim and peered through her veil, "Dad, what is a polite word for boogers?"

"Nose critters."

In perfect unison, Anna Grace and Hannah screeched, "Eeeeeeew!"

And just as Anna Grace turned to make a confident exit, Jennifer spoke. "Anna Grace. Hat — no. Heels — no."

"You want me to be a bag lady!"

With the sound of a truck horn, Thumper removed himself from Jennifer's feet and raced to the window, standing on hind legs, paws on the glass, and tail wagging. The Easter hat still on his head. Jim darted away and the three little sisters exited among shouts of, "Uncle Bird! Uncle Bird!"

"Bird" was Grandmother Jackie's nickname for her younger son, and that nickname made its way down to the next generation. Jennifer managed to grab the veiled hat from Anna Grace's head as the child bolted, unsteadily, on shiny black heels. Jennifer placed the hat on her own head and stared wistfully at her own image, for just a moment, before lowering the veil.

Jim cleared the front door just in time to see six-year-old JJ climb out of his dad's truck. JJ appeared to be prepared for all sorts of safari disasters; he wore a pith helmet on his little head and a pair of lighted binoculars swung 'round his neck. Jason stood beside his truck, checking his watch. Suddenly the screen door burst open a second time and the three girls poured, squealing, onto the lawn. Jennifer, hatless now, followed them onto the porch. The girls continued to whoop as they greeted JJ with hugs. The sisters loved their cousin JJ.

Jason shouted to Jim over the din, "C'mon, big brother; we need to pick up that Bobcat by two!"

As he made his way through the little crowd, Jim agreed, "Yeah, we don't wanna try to move that equipment on a weekday."

Jennifer waved from the porch. "Hey, Jason! Now you boys just run on. Kids, get outta the way. The zoo bus will be here any time now!"

At the mention of "zoo bus" JJ and his cousins began to whoop with joy.

Jason turned to his big brother just as he slid into the front seat. "Appreciate you doing this Jim. I know you got better things to do on a Saturday."

Still on the porch, Jennifer half smiled as she murmured, "Don't know what I'll do having the house all to myself." Then, as the truck pulled out of the drive, she yelled at the top of her lungs and windmilled her arms. "Y'all forgot — you forgot the *chili sauce.*"

But the brothers were gone. The four cousins watched until the truck disappeared and then craned their necks toward the bend in the road, hoping to hear the engine of the zoo bus. Jennifer watched them for a moment before speaking again. "You kids be safe and have a good time today. Ah — there's the phone! See y'all this evening."

Her voice was nearly lost beneath the squeal of kids and air brakes as the zoo bus pulled to a stop.

And with a swack of the screen door, Jennifer disappeared into the quiet house.

Miss Jenkins was not a school bus driver. No, she worked for the church and drove their bus for church functions like group picnics and bowling night and movies that showed you how to keep from going to hell. The kids considered her to be quite old, yet she kept her hair in pigtails like a little girl. She also wore old flip-flops on her feet, even in winter. Because today was a special day, she wore her good flip-flops with the rubber rose on top. Miss Jenkins reached out her hand and stopped the little figure in the huge pith helmet as he climbed onto her bus. "And who is that under the Jungle Jim hat?"

"It's me, Miss Jenkins. It's JJ Veitch."

In her bus-driver voice, she scolded, "You didn't bring any critters on board, did you?"

"Just nose critters," Patience offered, as she found her way to a seat. With a rubbery slap of the doors, the church bus was off.

The bus ride was an important part of any church outing. You were allowed to dress in short pants and see different sights from the everyday landscape. You could sit in any seat you wanted. And though the kids felt no compulsion to take advantage of this particular situation, Miss Jenkins would be one of only three adult supervisors until they reached their destination. As the bus sped along the two-lane, cows and horses received affectionate waves, shouts, and the occasional moo. Passing over the Chattahoochee River was particularly satisfying to the riders; due to recent rains the Hooch was leaping high on its banks. JJ had somehow managed to land a back seat, which everyone knows, is a prize. He did not waste his coveted location but began to write little greetings for the cars following them, and pressing them against the back glass. Most just ignored his work. But one car did toot its horn as it passed the bus, so they must have read the sign that said, "Honk if you like the zoo!"

Lightly trailing her hands along the backs of the seats on both sides of the aisle, Anna Grace made her way down the aisle mats to JJ's back-window position and asked, "JJ, where is Hannah?" JJ paused in the midst of drawing a brontosaurus (which he desperately hoped to see at the zoo) and looked at the backs of heads in front of him. And though he secretly loved taking care of the girls, he presented the obligatory sigh of irritation before rising and making his way up the aisle. By the time JJ reached the front, he felt a tightness in his throat. This wasn't like the big bus his mom and daddy had taken him on, which had its own little private restroom. There was no place to hide or be hidden. Where *was* Hannah?! His voice croaked a little when he first spoke. "Miss Jenkins —"

"JJ Veitch, you know you need to stay seated while this bus is in motion."

"Miss Jenkins. I can't find my cousin."

From the highway, the bus appeared to be slowing and pulling off to the side. But then, in a burst of noise and fumes, it knocked out a clean illegal U-turn, skittered across the grassy median, and sped off in the opposite direction.

In the late afternoon glow, the last of the kids were being escorted off the bus and onto Jim and Jennifer's lawn. Miss Jenkins was carefully checking a list, helped by a police officer. Already arriving were some of the parents, relieved to be picking up their own children and joining neighbors in offering advice and sympathy to Jim and Jennifer. Jason escorted his brother through the flashing lights and barking walkie-talkies, past a group of firemen to where a grey-haired police officer stood waiting for them. Neighbors moved in to console Jennifer.

Looking particularly small now, under the weight of his pith helmet and man-sized binoculars, JJ sat hunched on the porch, flanked by Patience and Anna Grace. After a moment, Patience turned to JJ and gently urged him to, "Make Hannah come home."

"She will, Patience, she will."

Anna Grace spoke for the first time since returning home. Her voice broke when she asked, "When? But when?"

JJ, knowing it was his job to take care of the girls, spoke soothingly. "By and by. Like in the song. Hannah will come home in the Sweet By and By."

Anna Grace shivered. "But what if it gets dark?"

"Is it dark in the Sweet By and By?" questioned little Patience.

No longer wanting to be in charge, JJ called for his mom twice; once quietly and again with vigor. Stephanie walked directly to the porch. "JJ, be still and quiet. Take the girls around back and play." JJ observed how serious his mom's face appeared.

Before bursting into sudden tears, Anna Grace managed, "We don't want to play. We want Hannah to come home."

Patience tuned up and sobbed with her sister. Stephanie sat down with the two red-faced girls and her bewildered son. "Girls, we want to bring Hannah home as soon as we can. And you can help by being quiet. Please don't worry. Go around and play on the swing set. Go play, and if you want to help Hannah, you can say a prayer for her to come home real soon. Why don't you go do that?"

Then she sent a conspiratorially significant look to JJ. As Stephanie re-joined the crowd, JJ manfully escorted his two cousins around the house to the back.

JJ took in the stilled swings and cold barbecue pit in the back yard and wondered how this was supposed to help. Away from the lights and noise of the front yard, and dappled by the setting sun, it was a pitiful lonesome sight. He was surprised at the cheery tone of his voice. "Come over here, Patience, and I'll push you in the swing!"

At first Patience made no sound, her face contorted and red, but then she cut loose with a full blown wail. A few startled birds left their tree perches and JJ rushed to his little cousin, unnerved by the sound. "Patience. Hey, remember what Mom said? We can say a prayer. Wanna do that? 'kay, come over here and put your hands in."

Yes, this was good. Doing something would keep them from thinking too much. With these thoughts to steady him, JJ led the girls to form their familiar prayer circle, with hands joined in the center. He remembered what his daddy had told him when he asked about the proper way to pray: "Just talk," Jason told him, "just talk to God like He is right here with you. Because He is." So JJ began to talk. "Dear Lord, Hannah got lost like a shepherd's lost lamb. Will You please find her and bring her home real quick? And will You help us to be good and not get in the way? And will You please — and thank You, Jesus. Anna Grace, why are you crying now?"

"Because there aren't enough hands! Look. We only have six hands." JJ looked down where he and his cousins held hands in the center of their prayer circle. Anna Grace continued, "When we say our prayers we always have eight. I want Hannah's hands to be here, too."

Patience snuffled, "I want Hannah's hands. I want to go look for Hannah!"

No longer crying, Anna Grace's voice sounded determined and spirited. "I want to go look for Hannah, too!"

"But Mom told us to stay right here! We can't go look. We'd get in big trouble!"

"JJ. We know places that Hannah might be that nobody else knows. Like our tree fort and the little rock stream in the woods. Let's go look in the woods!"

Patience agreed, "Look in the woods!"

"We can't." JJ was aware of feeling like he wanted to look in the woods, too. But he continued to protest. After all, he was in charge. "We're supposed to stay right here and we're going to stay right here!"

Anna Grace sounded totally logical as she calmly explained to JJ, "They're busy. We could find her and bring her back before they even know we're gone!"

And from Patience. "...even know we're gone..."

"JJ, she's lost!"

Patience added, "Like a shepherd's lamb."

Anna Grace stated simply, "I am going," as she turned away.

Patience bolted after her.

JJ weakly protested, "But...." and then dashed after the girls. The three little figures disappeared into the dim woods.

JJ, Anna Grace, and Patience moved slowly through the thick emerald air of the forest, calling Hannah's name. Late-day puddles of sunlight reached through the towering evergreens and caught and released them as they moved through. They had no idea how long they had been walking, when, as one, they stopped still and gazed at the gnarled woods that suddenly rose like a wall before them. "I don't recognize this part of the woods," Anna Grace half-whispered.

"Me neither," JJ replied, "we've never been this far before."

Determined to find Hannah, one by one they moved into the deep heart of the forest. In a blink, the atmosphere changed drastically. The trees and bushes moved in on the children and forced them to carefully avoid brambles and thorns, and crane their necks in order to see into the dimness. All three were still calling Hannah's name, but tentatively now.

Unable to walk steadily, the three found themselves crawling over fallen trees, under wrist-sized kudzu vines, and around rotting tree trunks. JJ's helmet gave him some protection against the sticky spider webs, while Anna Grace quickly learned to walk with one hand in front of her face to avoid the tacky wisps. Keeping the forest out of her face was the best she could do, as her hair and clothing were a mass of webs and dead leaves. Only able to see a few feet in front of them, they had no idea how far they had traveled, as the gathering gloom had moved in and blanketed the woods. Parting a particularly thick curtain of vines, JJ stopped. "Anna Grace, I really think we need to go back now. It'll be pitch dark by the time we get home."

"JJ, I just can't stand to think about Hannah all by herself, and…"

"What if she's not alone?" JJ tried to be encouraging. "Maybe she came back; maybe she's home."

"You might be right, but…"

"But what?"

"Which way is home?"

Breathing heavily, they tentatively looked around. Eyes wide, they couldn't seem to discern anything but indistinct forms. "Anna Grace, where's —"

JJ's question was interrupted by a high-pitched cry. Instantaneously, he was clawing and kicking at the darkness around him; leaping and crawling without giving any attention to reason. And just as quickly, he burst into an opening. A bit of twilight filtered through the trees and he began to cover the clearing at a fast run, trying not to lose the direction of the screams. And then he stopped dead. For a moment he rocked unsteadily, the light around his neck swinging wildly. JJ looked down into an even blacker darkness than the forest offered. His feet were perched at the edge of a black hole. "Patience? Patience?" From the depths came a thin, reedy cry. "Patience, are you hurt?"

A moment of deadly silence, and then Patience replied unsteadily, "JJ, I can't get out."

"Can you see me?"

"A little bit."

Anna Grace, forgotten for a moment, spoke from behind JJ. "That's a big hole!"

"That's not a hole. That's an old well." JJ lifted his binoculars and used the light to trace the round edges of the abandoned well. Placing his arm protectively in front of Anna Grace, he walked them both backward one step. Then he aimed his lamp downward. There, dirty but intact, was little Patience in her yellow jumpsuit. Anna Grace gasped, "We hafta get her out!"

"We can't get her out. We need help. Anna Grace, you're going to have to go back and get help."

"By myself?!"

"Yes. I can't leave Patience alone."

"Oh no, Hannah is lost and now Patience is trapped and I don't know how to get home."

There was real panic in Anna's voice. A whimper drifted up from the well. JJ's lamp was the only illumination now; night was upon them. He pointed the light down at Patience as he spoke calmly but firmly. "It's alright, Patience. I'm right here and I'm not gonna leave you. Just keep looking at my light. Anna Grace, you go right through thataway. You just go straight and keep going straight and you'll be alright. Purty soon your eyes will adjust and you'll be able to see by the moonlight. Just follow the moon. Then you bring everybody right back here. Tell them to holler real loud and I'll holler back. You can do this, Anna Grace."

She looked at JJ, lit from below by his lamp, and suddenly remembered how he held his flashlight below his chin when they told ghost stories. She wished they were around the campfire right now, with marshmallows. She wished — and then surprised herself when she abruptly turned and walked away. Long before Anna Grace disappeared back into the forest wall, JJ lost sight of her. He suddenly realized how cold it had grown.

Anna Grace was lost. After only a moment, the trees closed in overhead, and she lost sight of the moon. All around her were ominous shapes. Branches and leaves made crackling sounds all about. Still, she made her way through the brambles and vines, until something seemed to grab her foot and caused her to pitch forward, striking her head on a fallen tree. Anna Grace pulled herself up and climbed onto the tree and sat down. She pulled up her knees and wrapped her arms around them, so as to make herself as small as possible. She promised herself she wouldn't cry and for a long time, she didn't.

When Stephanie walked around the house to speak with JJ and the girls, she was grateful for a moment of quiet. And the back yard was, indeed, quiet. She looked carefully from one side of the yard to the other, and then opened her mouth to call out. Before making a sound, she stopped herself. She didn't want to overreact, or alarm those folks still in the front yard. Inwardly she was glad that the kids were inside the house, as it was growing quite cool. They were most likely getting something to eat. Eat! In all the madness she had forgotten to feed them!

Such good kids. Stephanie had long been aware of how blessed she was with children. She and Jason had lost their second child. She could still remember seeing Jackie holding the tiny bundle in her arms and whispering, "Breathe! Breathe!" It was not to be. They would have no more children. But they had JJ. As he grew, they did their best to instill in him a love for God and everything He gives us; to be kind and to be loving. But beyond these things, there was an innate goodness about him, and Stephanie saw this quality grow as he did. And her nieces! The girls were funny, creative, affectionate, and smart. Yes, she was blessed with all the children in her life. Even on this terrible night, JJ no doubt had the presence of mind to take the girls inside and see that they ate, so as not to be trouble. That was just like her boy.

Stephanie opened the back door expecting to smell popcorn or pizza. But there was nothing. The kitchen was empty and quiet. Of course! They were in the game room. She suddenly felt a need to hug JJ, and they wouldn't mind if she interrupted their video for a moment. She would later recall the odd sensation that made her hesitate before she pulled open the game room door.

Stephanie stood on the back deck, staring at the empty back yard and clutching the railing for support. She could see her short, quick breaths in the night air.

JJ could not tell how long Anna Grace had been gone. In the dark, time felt different. He had decided to save the battery on his light, and really thought their eyes might adjust to the darkness. But the trees would not allow the moonlight through and time dragged on in the blackness. He was singing to Patience; trying to keep her calm. He sang *In The Garden* and *What A Friend We Have In Jesus* and the theme song to Speed Racer. He started singing the theme from Gilligan's Island, but thought better of it, and sang the Bob the Builder song instead.

Feeling as if she might pass out, Stephanie held on to the railing as she descended the back deck. She had no idea what she was going to say or even if her mouth could form the needed words. This wasn't real; couldn't be real. "God help us now!" she whispered and began to walk around to the front of the house. She could hear the walkie-talkies and one of them seem to call to her, "Aunt Stephanie."

Stephanie turned around and saw a dim, dirty creature coming out of the woods.

A tiny light began to glow in the forest, small as a lightning bug. The light began to grow in size. Soon others joined it; glowing orbs floating in the night. A strong male voice called out, "Patience! JJ!"

Other voices joined in and other flashlights began to light the forest. In the bouncing yellow light pools, a fireman turned toward Jim and spoke to Anna Grace, who clung to Jim's neck. "Are you sure it was here?"

Anna Grace looked around as the fireman and her dad moved their lights about the trees. After a moment, she nodded. "Yes. I remember. It was right here. But JJ said he would wait. He said he'd holler back when he heard us calling. Where is he?"

Jim blurted out, "Wait! What was that? Over there!"

They all aimed their flashlights in the direction of Jim's pointing arm, but he snapped at them, "No! Turn your flashlights the other way; turn them off!"

The flashlights were cut and the group was pitched into blackness. There was no way to tell what was up or down, making it hard to keep balance or stand steady. Jim carefully lowered Anna Grace to the ground before speaking. "Look. There."

The darkness was revealing an eerie glow; seemingly coming up from the ground. The searchers moved cautiously toward it; Jim holding his daughter's hand. Drawing close, one by one, they stopped and stood at the boundary of the pale radiance. It was Jim who spoke first, "Patience? JJ?"

From the darkness below came a weak voice. "Uncle Jim?"

There at the bottom of the well, sat two lost lambs, barely lit by the failing battery in JJ's lamp.

In mere moments, the woods were lit like a circus midway. Walkie-talkies called in the other searchers, and fire and rescue workers tramped about. The forest looked bare and stark in the harsh lights, and yellow tape declared this was a place for CAUTION. Patience and JJ were seated on a big log, wrapped in blankets, and surrounded by their parents. One of the firemen motioned Jason aside before speaking in a low tone. "Mr. Veitch, I do have one question for your son before you take him home."

Jason and the fireman approached JJ; Jason seated himself close to JJ and spoke soothingly. "JJ, this nice man would like to ask you some questions. Go right ahead, sir."

The fireman removed his hat and spoke gently to the little boy on the log. "JJ, that other little girl told us that her sister was in the well, but she said you'd be waiting beside it. How did you end up down there, too?"

When JJ hesitated, Jason prodded, "Did you fall in?"

"No, sir."

"Then how did you end up down there?"

"I figured if God saw both of us down there, He would come get us twice as fast."

There seemed to be nothing else to say, and nothing was said until a loud animal screech cut through the forest. The screech must have prompted a thought in Anna Grace, who shouted, "Hannah! We forgot all about Hannah!"

Jim smiled. "Hannah's at home with Gommi and Poppi. She got home right after the three of you disobeyed us and got lost."

"Where was she?" JJ asked, "Where has Hannah been?"

Jim stood, lifting Patience and her blanket into his arms. "Let's head home and we'll tell you the story of Hannah and her adventure."

The family rose and, accompanied by the firemen, began to make their way through the forest. Perhaps it was the oddly magical backdrop of the night forest, or the sudden release of tension, or maybe it was Jim's innate story-telling ability that brought the saga to life. And in stories, as we all know, anything can happen.

Chapter Two

A Thumper, a New Friend, and a Book

J im began to set the scene, thusly, "When you kids jumped on the zoo bus, the phone started ringing and Jennifer ran in to catch it. What she didn't realize was..."

Jennifer stood on the porch waving goodbye to the kids. "You kids be safe and have a good time today. Ah — there's the phone! See y'all this evening."

Her voice was nearly lost beneath the squeal of the kids and the zoo bus brakes. And she didn't even realize that Thumper had taken advantage of all the distractions to slip skillfully and silently out the screen door, knocking off his Easter hat in the process.

So with the swack of the door, Jennifer disappeared into the quiet house.

Thumper scampered across the lawn, but paused before he sped off into The World. He looked back and was delighted to see no one chasing or calling him. Thumper chuckled gleefully, "I'm free! I'm free! Dum-da-dum-dum-dum! I'm free! And I'm *naked!*"

And with his nose high in the air and his tail wagger set on highest speed, he cut through a neighbor's yard and began his adventure.

Hannah, the last to climb aboard the zoo bus, witnessed the escape, and bolted after Thumper. However, her cry of, "Wait!" was lost in the chug of the bus motor and the sound of forty screaming kids.

Miss Jenkins did not hear Hannah, nor did she see her disembark from the bus. No, Miss Jenkins pulled the door shut and headed off to the zoo.

Walking through the night woods, Jim continued his story with, "Hannah must have thought Miss Jenkins saw her and would wait for her."

Running down the sidewalk after Thumper, a thought bubble appeared over Hannah's head: "That's right, Dad; I thought Miss Jenkins saw me and would wait." And then Hannah cried, "Thumper! Thumper!"

Meanwhile Thumper, safely ahead of Hannah, took the time to express his delight over a strange-smelling lawn with manicured shrubbery. He giggled as only hounds can and declared, "I can pee here and I can pee here and I can pee there — woooops, better run faster!"

Jim: "Hannah finally gave up and returned to find the bus gone."

Hannah: "The bus is gone!"

Jim: "Imagine how surprised she must have been."

Hannah: "Yes. Imagine how surprised I must be!"

A rattletrap car demanded Hannah's immediate attention. The car was painted with flowers and Bible verses, and Miz Gribble was all gussied up in a wild hat and overalls. She stuck her head out the window and addressed Hannah: "Are you waiting for the zoo bus, Hannah Veitch?"

"No, Miz Gribble, the bus is already gone and I missed it!"

"Well, I'm headed over to the zoo to help watch you kids. Hop in!"

"Well, maybe I should just —"

"Now, Hannah Veitch, you just jump right in my auto and I bet we'll beat the bus to the zoo."

Jim: "Hannah must have known this was a stupid thing to do as soon as she did it."

Hannah: "I do. I really do."

Jim: "Meanwhile, Thumper must have been having quite a time, doing just as he pleased."

Thumper: "I am. I really am." And he peed on another bush.

Jim: "And as Miz Gribble's car coughed, revved up and picked up speed, Hannah at least tried to do the right thing."

Hannah: "Miz Gribble, can you please call my mom? Just in case someone notices I'm missing?"

Miz Gribble: "Hannah Veitch, I lived my entire life without having to carry a telephone around with me and I'm not gonna start now. Besides, we'll be at the zoo before you can say *souse on a cracker!*"

Jim: "Miz Gribble's a sweet lady, but she thinks cell phones are the work of the devil."

Miz Gribble: "And so are pant suits, reality shows, and public restrooms!"

Jim: "Meanwhile, JJ discovered that Hannah was missing and Miss Jenkins turned the bus around and headed home."

The bus, now wearing a colorful cartoon face, reached out with its front wheels and dug into the pavement, causing its back end to rear up into the air. Little cartoon kids rolled forward with thumps and screams. The cartoon bus then raised itself up on long, tall tire-legs and walked daintily over the median, holding up its skirts as it did, settled onto the opposite side of the road, and took off with a blast of smoke. The little cartoon kids rolled to the back with more bumps and cries.

Nearing the house, Jim was winding up his story, "By the time Miz Gribble drove all around the zoo parking lot looking for the bus, then drove all the way back here with Hannah, the bus had returned and unloaded and you kids were off into the woods."

There before the exhausted family and the loyal firemen and police officers, rose the Jim Veitch home. It looked especially inviting with all the windows radiating a golden hue that reached out and lit the back lawn.

Suddenly the back door burst open and Jackie and Larry Carpenter crossed out onto the deck. JJ and the girls knew Jackie and Larry as their Gommi and Poppi, but Jim and Jason had not always known Larry as their father. However, Larry had become more than grandfather and father to this family. He was a quiet man who was slow to anger, and more than once diffused an argument with his gentle humor. Jackie, gregarious and sociable, and the retiring Larry, made an odd, yet perfect couple. And to Jackie and the rest of the family, Larry had become their rock.

Abruptly Hannah darted from the house and between her grandparents and, taking the deck steps two at a time, bolted into the arms of her cousin and sisters. Jackie and Larry joined in the chaotic celebration, with Jackie making sure each fireman and police officer received a firm hug. After the noise began to ebb, and a few nightgown'd and pajama'd neighbors dropped by to express their joy, Jackie raised her voice in the chill night air: "Alright, now, let's get everybody inside. Hot chocolate!"

Jason protested mildly that they might oughta get JJ on home, but before they could make an exit, Anna Grace spoke up: "Wait. I want all the hands."

Jim questioned his daughter, "What, Honey?"

JJ understood and explained, "Anna Grace wants us to say our prayer. Now that we got all our hands back."

One by one, the young people formed their little circle in the pool of light pouring from the house. Eight little hands were now joined in the middle of their circle. JJ spoke first, "Thank You, Jesus, for bringing home our little lost lamb, Hannah."

Hannah followed, "Thank You, God, for leading the police and firemen through the woods and the night."

Anna Grace added, "And thank You for rescuing JJ and Patience from the deep, dark well."

Finally, Patience spoke up, "And thank You for bringing us all back home, in the Sweet By and By."

The faces of the adults expressed what words never could say. Gently the kids broke free and the family members began to move, as if in slow-motion, toward the warm light of home. From a distance, Patience' voice was heard: "Where's Thumper?"

On February 28 of 2008, JJ, Hannah, Anna Grace, and Patience walked down the sidewalks that crisscrossed their subdivision. Anna Grace was inexplicably wearing an apron bearing the words, *Kiss the Cook!,* set off by pearl earrings and a tiara. The incident at the well, just five days earlier, was practically forgotten on that chilly afternoon, because the kids had a vital task ahead of them. As they passed a lamppost, Hannah took the top leaflet from the stack she carried in her book bag. Still in his school uniform, JJ produced a large stapler and attached the flyer to the pole at all four corners. Now another photo of a smiling Thumper announced to the neighborhood that he was lost. Anna Grace looked into the big brown eyes before joining the others. Swallowing a lump in her throat, she spoke, "Thumper always came home before."

"He'll come back again," Hannah assured her.

"But it's been so long. Almost a week."

"I told you he'll come home. These signs will help."

"How?" asked Patience mournfully, "Thumper can't even read."

Jason's voice startled them. They were so intent on finding Thumper that the little band had not even noticed Jason's truck slowing to a stop. Jason leaned across the seat and spoke through the open window, "Hey, kids; I'm going out to the construction site. Wanna come?"

"No, thanks, Uncle Bird," Hannah answered, "We have to put up all these signs for Thumper."

"Ya sure you don't want a little break? I'm stopping by the hardware store."

The hardware store was catnip to JJ and he slapped the stapler into Anna Grace's hands and turned toward his dad's truck. "Cool. Hardware!" Hesitating, he squelched his sudden joy and, turning back to the girls, stated solemnly, "I'll stay if you need me."

Hannah spoke up, "No, thanks; we can put up the rest."

With a grin and a leap, JJ was in the front seat, buckling his seat belt. Before he drove off, Jason reminded the girls, "Now you all be careful! And we'll keep our eyes open for Thumper. Here, give me one of those signs for the hardware store."

No thrill ride at the county fair could compare with Arliss' Hardware. Not in JJ's eyes. Before Jason could come to a full stop, his son was peering through the windshield, mesmerized. Why, you hardly even needed to go inside! Under the striped outdoor canopy, the old store beckoned to shoppers with things that glittered and whirled and shimmied. You could make your way through a shiny sea of garden tools and giddily waving sale signs to the working, real (but with fake birds) birdbaths, and climb upon clean, green riding mowers. There were bags of fertilizer to sniff and racks of tiny tomato plants to stroke and always some gadget that your daddy might buy for you because it was broken or didn't cost much. Jason cut the engine and hit the concrete with a whomp of his work boots. As Jason entered the big doors, propped open with outdoor grills that were ON SALE, JJ slid out of the truck and, still without blinking, entered into the sights and smells and feels of the big, shady front porch of this local wonderland. JJ glanced up through the show windows and saw his dad inside talking to Arliss, both slouched against an end cap bearing colorful seed packets.

"Arliss, I've done all I know. I got these *Smile, you're on camera!* signs all over the place, but I figure a few more won't hurt."

Arliss commiserated as he placed some stray seed packets back in their proper slot. "Jason, these copper thieves are holding us all hostage. One cut phone line and you got a whole neighborhood without phone, internet; no security systems..."

"But they're cleaning me out! I get a house half built and they strip it! They hit the houses soon as we got the plumbing and electrical installed, and each house costs me about six thousand dollars to refurnish. Arliss, they hit me sixteen times on this one site alone."

"You don't mean it!"

"And my deductable is too high, so it comes out of my pocket."

Arliss turned his full attention to Jason now. "Can't the police help you out?"

"Well, that's what we're about to find out. Meeting a county officer out there in about a half hour. He's s'posed to give me some advice."

"You let me know what you find out."

"I will. Wood stakes down this a'way?"

"Yeah, just this side of gardening."

Meanwhile, JJ had worked his way inside the store and was perusing the aisles, top to bottom. Jason turned and walked down the aisle toward gardening, just barely missing three drywall workers who crossed the head of the aisle behind him.

These three workers were named Jose Lerma, Ernesto Morales, and Juan Carlos Reymundo. Jason would meet them very soon, but he would not know their names until much later.

JJ was fascinated by something out of his reach. He stood, tip-toe, and began to climb up the shelving, balanced precariously by his toes and fingers. Catching him out of the corner of his eye, Jose Lerma halted at the head of the aisle and watched. Suddenly JJ's foot slipped, leaving him hanging only by his fingers. In an instant, Lerma dashed over and grabbed JJ, gently lowering him to the ground. Jose Lerma spoke in a way that sounded strange to JJ. "Hey you should more being careful. Things on top only are for big people."

JJ stared at him, then at the prize on the top shelf. It was a collection of model trucks, each bearing the proud logo *Arliss Hardware*. Lerma quizzed JJ again, "What you try to reach? Is it this? No? That? No? You want this roofing nails?"

JJ shook his head and stared up. Lerma's eyes lit up. "Ah, I see what you are wanting. This, huh?" Lerma pulled one of the trucks off the top shelf and placed it in JJ's hands.

At last JJ spoke, "Thank you."

"Okay then. So you are being careful and don't be getting hurt."

JJ grinned. "Okay."

Reappearing at the end of the aisle, Morales barked at Lerma, "Apurate, Jose. Que estas haciendo?"

Reymundo added hastily, "Si, apurate; vas hacer que lleguemos tarde!"

Lerma leaned down and whispered to JJ, "Be. Careful."

Jose Lerma grinned and walked away to join his friends. The three men disappeared around the corner, exactly one second before Jason turned down that same aisle to pick up JJ.

Jason sped onto his construction site, truck tires kicking up red dust. Landscaping wouldn't begin on this subdivision until the houses were completed, which he hoped would be soon. Until they could find a way to stop the copper thieves, the workers were stalled at one phase of the building process, endlessly repeating. As the dust cleared, Jason spotted a Crockett County police vehicle parked near one of the houses. Good! At last he would have some professional advice! Jason leaned over and addressed JJ. "I want you to wait here while I go talk to this policeman. Then you can go over and inspect the houses with me. 'kay?"

JJ looked up at his dad and smiled a quick, "'kay" before returning his attention to his new truck.

Jason reached over JJ and rolled down his window, hopped out of the truck and slammed the door shut. His boots made little red clouds each time they dug into the clay. As he approached the patrol car, he spied a compact, muscular figure seated on the hood. Jason threw up his hand. The officer looked over the top of his mirrored sunglasses and addressed Jason. "You Jason Veitch?

"Yes, sir."

"Book. Officer Clayton Book. Crockett County Police Department."

Officer Book slid off the hood and leaned against the car, arms crossed. "I hear you been having a little trouble with copper thieves."

Leaning on a dusty sawhorse, Jason laughed, "Way more than a little trouble. And I've tried 'bout everything I know."

Book removed his glasses and stared straight at Jason. "Mr. Veitch, what steps have you taken to stop these thefts yourself?"

"Well, I put up some signs — see, over there — and I left my vehicle here overnight, hoping they might think somebody was still here and —"

"Whoa, whoa, whoa! Mr. Veitch, you're not gonna make a dent in these people with signs. These copper thieves are modern day pirates."

At the word "pirates" JJ sat up, immediately attentive, and leaned out the window.

Book continued in a sure manner, "...and pirates only understand one thing: Force. Force of the law and force of ownership. You wanna put a stop to this right quick?"

"Yes, sir, I'd sure like to."

"Then here's what you do: You hire you a bunch o' teenage boys. Have 'em spend the night out there in them woods, and just pounce and beat the crap out of 'em. Come daylight, the teenage boys just disappear and so do the copper thieves. Nothing speaks louder than a busted head."

"Ah, no, I wouldn't feel comfortable doing that. What if one of them boys got hurt or —"

"Mr. Veitch do you own a firearm?"

"No. Well, I guess so. I gotta couple old guns my daddy had, but I've never even fired a gun."

"That's okay, you won't need to fire 'em. Just plant yourself in them woods tonight. I'll have my men patrolling this area all night. All you gotta do at the first hint of suspicious behavior is call 911 and my men will be here in a matter of seconds."

JJ leaned his chin on the door and continued to listen. In case the policeman said something else about pirates.

Chapter Three

Pirates Change Everything

J J was dreaming about pirates. They had his daddy tied up on their ship and JJ was trying to catch up in a little tiny boat that looked like a toy truck. The sun was so bright that it was hard for JJ to see which direction he should be going. He shut his eyes, shielded them with his hand and then re-opened them. The bright light was the overhead light in his room. Uncle Jim and Aunt Jennifer were standing over his bed. They were both wearing coats over pajamas. Upon seeing him open his eyes, Uncle Jim went over to the closet and pulled out JJ's coat and shoes. Aunt Jennifer sat on the edge of his bed and began to speak quietly. "Hey, Sweetie. You busy sleeping?"

He wanted to ask her why they were in his room and to tell them about the pirates, but all that came out was, "Mmmm-hmmmm."

"How'd you like to come over and spend the rest of the night with me and Uncle Jim and the girls?"

"Where's my mama and deddy?"

"Oh, your mama's right out there in the kitchen."

Jim began to wrap JJ in his coat. He smiled as he spoke to his little nephew. "And the girls are out in the car waiting for you."

JJ was growing more confused. "What for?"

Jim lifted him out of bed and whispered into his ear, "C'mon. It'll be an adventure."

As the three hurried down the darkened hallway, JJ spotted his mama in the kitchen and reached out for her. For some reason she turned her back on him before she spoke. "You run on, now, Honey, and have fun. Mama'll see you in the morning."

Just before they left the house, JJ called, "Deddy?"

Jennifer opened the back door of their vehicle. The interior light sprang on and JJ could see in the back seat, Hannah, Anna Grace, and Patience, all in pajamas. Patience was sleeping soundly, leaning up against Anna Grace, who, like Hannah, had a strange look on her face. Jennifer closed the back door, then opened the passenger door and got in next to Jim without saying a word. Hannah put her arm protectively around JJ as the car sped away. Just before his house was out of sight, JJ looked out to see his mama standing on the porch. She was holding her hand over her mouth.

As Jim's car pulled into Jason's sunny yard the next morning, JJ could see there were several cars in the drive. He looked toward the front porch, half expecting to see his mama standing there, just as he had left her last night. He climbed out of the car and began to walk toward the front door. It felt odd to be wearing his pajamas in the daytime. But for the moment, he just wanted to get inside and see his mama and daddy and feel normal again.

When JJ stepped inside his house, it took a moment for his eyes to adjust from the bright sunlight. In the darkness, he was reminded about his pirate dream and felt a sharp need to see his daddy. He could now make out that his Gommi and Poppi were seated, as was his mom. No one stood; they just stared at JJ with funny looks, like they tasted something bad. Someone was standing with his back to JJ and talking to his family. JJ caught part of it: "....gotta understand that I am just Jason's real-estate attorney. I'm in way over my head on this."

Abruptly the man stopped talking and turned to face JJ. It was Mr. Ellis. Mr. Ellis was a friend of his parents and helped them with things like signing papers. When Ellis Burdette saw JJ, he got that funny look on his face and stammered, "Oh. I —"

Larry gestured to JJ and waved him over. "Come over here and say hi to Poppi, Little Man."

At the same time, Jackie waved him her way. "JJ, come give Gommi a hug."

Warily, JJ crossed to Jackie and he spoke as she hugged him. "Where's Deddy?"

Jackie looked down at her hands for a moment before speaking. "Sugar. Your daddy has...had an accident."

Now JJ knew all about accidents. He used to have accidents when he drank too much before bedtime, but he hadn't had one in ages. And he couldn't imagine a grownup having an accident. While he was pondering this strange turn of events, Stephanie began to sob. Before he could ask his mom what was wrong, Ellis stepped up and addressed him. "JJ, do you remember your daddy talking to you about copper thieves?"

"Yes, sir. They're like pirates."

Ellis smiled. "Yep. I guess they are. Well, those thieves were taking all your daddy's copper and he couldn't build houses. So he tried to stop them. And there was an accident with a gun. And one of them got killed. Now some folks think it was your daddy's fault, and until they find out for sure that it was just an accident, Jason has to stay with them."

"At their house?"

"No, sir; in jail."

"Jail?"

Jackie broke in. "Yes, but Ellis and — and some friends of Ellis — are going to make sure the people at the jail find out the truth, and send your daddy on back to us."

JJ was confused on so many levels. He wondered how you could have an accident with a gun. He wondered what pirates wanted with copper. But most of all he wondered, because of his dream about pirates stealing his daddy, if he was somehow responsible for all this strangeness. The only thing he knew for sure, was that his daddy was not here. Without a word, JJ bolted and ran into his room. After a moment, Ellis came in and sat beside him on the bed. "JJ. That's a cool car."

"It's a truck."

"Where'd ya get it?"

"My deddy bought it for me."

"When?"

"Yesterday."

"Do anything else yesterday?"

"Yes, sir."

"What was that?"

"Went to my deddy's construstion site."

"Did you help your daddy with his houses?"

"No, sir; I just sat in the car."

"What did Daddy do?"

"Talked to the police."

Ellis shifted and leaned in a bit. "Did you see them?"

"Yes, sir."

"Did you hear them?"

"Yes, sir."

"What did they talk about?"

"Catching copper pirates."

"Do you remember what the policeman told your daddy? Think hard."

JJ put down his truck and brought up the memory of sitting in the car, his head leaning out the window, listening to the police man talk to his daddy. "He told my deddy to hire some boys to beat up the pirates."

Ellis took a short breath. "Do you remember anything else he said?"

"He told my deddy to hide in the woods with a gun and when they tried to steal his copper to call him. And he said he'd tell the other police to stay real close all night, so they could come right over and arrest the men taking my deddy's stuff."

Ellis sat quietly for a moment. Then he addressed JJ again. "You sure got a great memory, JJ. That's exactly what your daddy told us. Tell you what: I'm going back in the living room to talk to your mom. But I'll see you real soon. And JJ. Your daddy is real proud of you."

Ellis stood to leave, but stopped at JJ's voice. "Mr. Ellis. Did I do good?"

"You sure did."

"Then will you go get my deddy now?"

That very same morning, the morning of Jason's arrest, Larry drove Jackie and Stephanie to the jail. There they were directed to a crowded, noisy, waiting area with buzzing, blinking fluorescent lights. There seemed to be no way to get away from the noise and stale air and both Larry and Jackie, who were seated on each side of a near-catatonic Stephanie, were constantly touched, rubbed, and jostled by other bodies. A thought began to weigh heavily on Larry's mind: If it was this bad here, what might it be like for Jason?

After an agonizingly long wait, an officer strutted into the room and snapped some orders. Larry nudged Jackie and drew her attention to the red, plastic, letter "A" that she was gripping. They had been summoned. The A-Group followed the officer down a long hallway. On each side, prisoners who were mopping or sweeping or carrying clean linens backed up to the walls and ducked their heads as the group passed.

Finally they were led into a phone booth. At least, that's what Stephanie thought it was. Yes, it was small and there was a phone and a little metal seat. But there was also a window with obscenities scratched into the hard plastic. The coffin-like area allowed only enough room for Stephanie to sit. Larry and Jackie stood, the walls of the coffin pressing in on them. The smell was terrible and Jackie tried not to think about what might be causing it. They could see the prisoners being led in on the other side of the murky windows. And one of them was Jason. He was in a red jumpsuit; as they would later learn, red for murderer. When Jason saw his family, he burst into convulsive sobs. He was speaking rapidly, trying desperately to convey something to Stephanie. But they could not hear him until Jackie gestured for him to pick up the phone on his side. This was the image they had to carry home with them: their husband/son locked away from them, broken and terrified.

Also on that morning, Jim somehow had the presence of mind to think about checking on Jason's houses. He didn't know why he felt the need, perhaps there was some clue there to help them comprehend this baffling turn of events. Or maybe it was just the fact that Jason might ask about his houses. He'd worked so hard and spent so much money trying to protect his property and make a living. It was the least Jim could do to check on Jason's new subdivision. When Jennifer convinced Jim that he, instead, should stay with his girls and near their home phone, he called on their cousin Dennis. Dennis was even closer to the site and was grateful to be doing something to help. Dennis grew increasingly tense as he neared the development and realized he would be standing where, just a few hours earlier, one life ended and another life was changed forever. As he turned into the subdivision, the first thing he noticed was a Crockett County police car. Yellow crime scene tape was fluttering in the breeze and three men stood on Jason's property. One man was a short, muscular police officer. The other two were dark-skinned civilians with black hair. Dennis was almost certain he knew the identity of these three men; he had been briefed on the incident of the previous day and night, and this looked mighty suspicious. Dennis approached the three and addressed them, "Excuse me, but this is private property. Can I ask what you're doing here?"

The officer, wearing sunglasses and a name tag that identified him as Officer Book, strolled over and right up to Dennis, and spoke through a grin, "We're waiting for our attorney and the Channel 32 news truck. These two gentlemen watched their friend get murdered in cold blood last night and we're going to make sure the public knows about it." Book's grin faded as he continued, "And exactly who are you?"

"I'm Jason Veitch's cousin and co-owner of this property. And if you want the public to know what happened, then I'll make sure to tell the TV cameras Jason's side of the story as well."

The two black-haired men were speaking in Spanish and Book just stared. Dennis wished he could see the man's eyes, but the officer's mirrored lenses only reflected Dennis's own face. After making his intentions clear, Dennis calmly walked back to his car.

It was only then that Dennis realized he was shaking. And he wondered if he could get into trouble for lying to a police officer and saying he was co-owner of the property. Never mind. He'd made his point. Jason couldn't speak for himself. So Dennis did instead. And he didn't regret lying to the officer at all. Apparently lying was something this officer was quite used to.

Chapter Four

Bullies

A few days later at the Jim Veitch home, three little girls were running up the sidewalk toward the house. Hannah, Anna Grace, and Patience shouted in unison and at the top of their lungs, "Daddy!" as they crossed the yard and burst through the front door.

Their parents seemed to be in deep conversation, but Jennifer leapt to her feet quickly and asked in a voice almost as breathless as the girls, "What is it; what happened?!"

"We found Thumper!"

Looking a teeny bit like a mama duck with her little ones, Jim marched down the sidewalk with his three little ducklings behind him, racing to keep up. Jim had a look of concern and determination on his face that Hannah had rarely seen, and she knew it wasn't only Thumper on her dad's mind. Struggling to keep up in a pair of oversized ballet slippers and with a tutu over her jeans, Anna Grace gasped, "Will you rescue Thumper?"

Hannah didn't even turn. "Of course he will, Anna Grace."

"And will he come home today?"

"Yes, Anna Grace. Daddy can do anything."

Patience, red-faced from running, could only manage, "And after you get Thumper...."

Jim, still marching, "Yes, Pay-Pay?"

"...will you bring Uncle Bird home, too?"

Jim began to slow down, hovering at the mouth of a side street; ragged and run-down. This was a distinctly different part of town. The girls gathered close to their father. Together, they began to walk down the buckled pavement. Hannah took Pay-Pay's hand as they made the final turn and stopped before the gate of a weathered dwelling. An old chain-link fence slouched around the bare dirt yard. A sign on the gate warned KEEPOUT; another on the front door announced this was PRIVATE PROPATY. On the mailbox was the single name *Vertue*. And chained to an old, dead tree, pacing uneasily, was Thumper. At the site of his family, Thumper stood statue still. Jim called out to the owner, then glanced reassuringly at the girls. Thumper moaned deep in his chest as the front door opened with a protesting screech, revealing a leathery man in soiled work clothes. Without looking at Jim, he walked up to him.

"Morning, Mr. Vertue."

Mr. Vertue nodded and shifted the chaw in his mouth.

"Mr. Vertue, my name's Jim Veitch and these are my girls and that dog back there is their dog. We thank you for finding him and taking care of him and we'll take him home with us now."

Mr. Vertue cocked his head toward a pale boy who'd been hovering behind the shell of a rusty Ranchero. "S'my boy's dog."

Still amiable, Jim replied, "Sir, I believe my girls told you this morning that he belongs to us. Now we're here to take him home."

Mr. Vertue turned toward the boy. "Travis, where'd you git this dog?"

"Told you, Pop, I found him at the dump last Halloween."

Vertue turned back to Jim with a glint of smug satisfaction in his eye. "S'my dog. Not yours."

And then something happened that seemed very strange, at least to the girls. Some other man's voice suddenly came out of Jim. They knew their daddy better than anyone, but for a moment, he seemed to be possessed by the spirit of someone else, and his voice was like the old motor oil that daddy drained out of the car; all slick and burned black. His words streamed very fast. "Mr. Vertue, our dog has a microchip under his skin. All I have to do is call our vet and he will scan that chip and it will prove that he is our dog. But if you force me to do that, then I'll have to call the law, too. So what you think I should do now, Mr. Vertue?"

Without further ado, Mr. Vertue walked toward Thumper and unclipped the chain around his neck. Before Jim could even open the gate, Thumper bounded toward his little mistresses, and jumped the fence. For a while, they were all lost in a joyful, jumping, slobbery reunion. Then Hannah attached Thumper's leash and they began to walk toward home, feeling like they were floating several inches above the road. With the Vertue place safely behind them, Hannah looked back. Mr. Vertue was nowhere to be seen. Travis was standing in the road, watching them until they were out of sight.

Like many six-year olds, JJ was easily distracted. He had arrived at his grandparents' house with his overnight bag and a heavy heart. JJ wanted to see his daddy. But several hours at Gommi and Poppi's house had lifted his mood. He always looked forward to "the big house" and its swimming pool and endless treats and videos and games. Jackie and JJ were sprawled across her four-poster bed, which was littered with colorful rubber and plastic figures. JJ was explaining the proper use, care, and feeding of dinosaurs. This was a serious subject, as his solemn voice denoted. "And I'll let you borrow these for tonight."

"So, I have to keep these dinosaurs in my bed tonight?" Jackie was paying close attention.

JJ laughed, "*No, Gommi*, you have to keep them *beside* the bed to keep monsters from getting *in* the bed."

Jackie, wide-eyed, "Ohhhhhhhh."

"And if you have to go to the bathroom in the night, don't step on them. That's how this one got his tail broke."

"Don't you and your mommy need to put some beside your bed tonight?"

"No, because, see the monsters don't know that we're here! How come are we sleeping at your house tonight?"

"So we can get up real early tomorrow and go to the courthouse. Gommi's house is closer than yours."

"And the courthouse is where my deddy gets his ears checked?"

"Get his — what's that mean, JJ?"

"Uncle Jim said everybody was going to the courthouse for my deddy's hearing."

"That's a...it's a....different kind of hearing, JJ. This is where a bunch of people *hear* what really happened with your daddy. And when they see it was really an accident, they'll let your daddy come home."

"Can I come hear, too?"

"Oh, I don't think you would like it. It's real dull and serious. So after me and Poppi and your mama get up and get dressed, Aunt Jennifer is gonna come over and bring the girls. And all five of you are gonna grill out and play games and eat anything you want."

Stephanie padded into the room, wearing her pajamas. "But right now, you need to get some sleep, Sugar."

Jackie inquired, "Larry?"

"Asleep in his easy chair."

The women laughed and Jackie pulled JJ close. "You come give Gommi some sugar."

Stephanie smoothed his hair. "You wanna say your prayers for your grandmother before we go to bed?"

Without further prompting, JJ slipped to the floor and knelt on the soft tufted rug, clasping his little hands and lowering his head. "Dear Jesus, thank You for the trees and for food and for cable TV and for sunshine. Please bless all my family and all my friends and all the little animals and help me to be good and get good grades. And most of all, thank You for letting my deddy come home tomorrow. Amen."

It felt as if they had been in the little room for hours. There were no windows, and except for a wooden table and six chairs, no furnishings. No flag or clock, just industrial-green walls. The family had arrived early for the preliminary hearing, and Stephanie, Jim, Larry, and Jackie were sequestered in an unused deliberation room until time for proceedings to begin. When the frosted glass doorway finally rattled open, everyone jumped. A court officer briefed them and told them to follow her. Jackie held her Bible close as the little band rose and walked through corridor after corridor that all looked the same.

The sound coming from the wooden double doors alerted them that the courtroom was packed. They walked into a smallish, stuffy, crowded courtroom with a low ceiling. And as they were escorted to the empty first row, the room became completely quiet. Within seconds of having the reserved sign removed and seating themselves, an officer announced the entrance of the judge. It had begun.

That same morning found JJ and the girls romping in the early spring sunlight. The back deck of Jackie and Larry's house extended to the pool, and beyond the crystal blue water and pastel deck chairs, the landscape rose in gently tiered acreage toward the distant treeline. Jennifer watched the children from the deck, mobile phone pressed to her ear, listening to every word that Jim said.

Jim spoke quietly but urgently into his phone. Behind him, members of the court, the press, and his own family spilled loudly out of the courtroom and into the hallway, making him wonder if Jennifer could hear what he had to say. Reluctantly, he raised his voice, "Jennifer! He's not coming home; Jason's not coming home. They charged him with felony murder and took him back to jail. We have to bail him out. Jen, they took him out in chains and..."

Spotting Jennifer on the phone, JJ bolted toward the deck. As he came within hearing range, he shouted, "Deddy? Is that my deddy?" Jennifer interrupted Jim with a simple, "I gotta go now."

Jennifer lowered the phone and ushered a panting JJ into the house. Hannah stopped playing and stood still, watching, as Jennifer closed the door.

The clock on the piano showed 2:42. JJ and Stephanie sat on the piano bench staring alternately at the phone and the clock. It was a little crystal and gold clock, a wedding present to Stephanie and Jason. She tried hard to remember who had given it to them. Stephanie had initially been grateful for the suggestion to remain home while bail was posted. She had felt terribly weak after the disturbing turn of events in the courtroom earlier that day. But now she wondered if she had made the right choice. Sitting and waiting was stressing her to the limit. She kept picturing Jason trying to keep up with the guards, shackles on his feet, as they took him away. 2:43 now. She willed the phone to ring. Nothing. JJ shifted on the bench, making a sharp creaking sound that almost covered the first ring. With the sound of that first ring still hanging in the air, Stephanie had the phone in her hand. "Jackie?"

Jackie had her hand cupped around the phone, to cut down on the noise in the bail bonds agency. "Stephanie, listen. We paid his bond but they won't release Jason until they pick up some items from his office. Now the lead investigator's name is Gus Crutcher, and..." Jackie glanced up at Larry, who was filling out forms with Crutcher's help. "...and Mr. Crutcher is going to follow us over to your house as soon as all the paper work is done. Steph, we have to get all this taken care of and get back to the jail by five or they'll keep Jason another night! Do you know where Jason's passport is?" Jackie spotted Larry and Crutcher moving rapidly toward her with Larry nodding affirmatively. "Never mind, Stephanie; we're on our way."

Stephanie did not hear that last part. With JJ in tow, she had already dashed down the hall to Jason's office.

Jason always preferred lamp light in his office, as it was a home office and the soft light kept the homey feel. But on this late afternoon, even the sunlight was obliterated by the harsh fluorescent overheads, a holdover from when this room had been part of the garage. Jackie and Stephanie stood rigidly against the paneled wall as Gus Crutcher explored Jason's office. Crutcher reminded Stephanie of a mannequin at the Suit Shack; he was sleek and un-creased and his face didn't move when he spoke. Dispassionately and efficiently, he pulled drawers, opened cabinets, and slid his fingers into nooks. To Crutcher, he was just doing his job, but to Jackie and Stephanie, it was more like a home invasion. He was fast and merciless as he tossed files, photos, and folders into plastic containers. Without slowing, he inquired, "Passport?"

Stephanie's arm jerked to attention and pointed as she spoke, "Ah — oh — it's in the...top middle drawer; I put it there so you could —" Crutcher snapped open the drawer and flipped open Jason's passport, then tossed it into a container. "— find it without any trouble," Stephanie finished lamely.

Crutcher had pulled a manila file from the depths of a drawer and loose pages cascaded out and onto Jason's desk. Picking them up, Crutcher began to examine each page carefully. "Oh, those are just Jason's sermons," Stephanie explained. "He's studying for the ministry. Was. Studying..."

"Do you have to take those?" Jackie asked.

Crutcher stuffed the sermons back into the file, and returned them to the cabinet. He continued his search.

"Please, Mr. Crutcher," Stephanie spoke desperately, "it's after four o'clock."

"Does your husband keep any weapons in his office?"

"No, he has an old handgun from the Spanish Civil War that my daddy —"

"Where?"

"He keeps it in that cabinet behind you."

Crutcher brusquely turned and jerked open the cabinet doors. A framed photo on the cabinet top fell face forward with a metallic bang. Crutcher righted the photo and then, with his hand remaining on it, became oddly still. He gazed at the picture of JJ kneeling beside his bed, hands clasped in prayer. Suddenly a little voice piped up from behind, "Are you gonna take my deddy's picture?"

Crutcher, still holding the photo, turned to see JJ framed in the doorway. JJ moved forward and indicated the picture. "See, my deddy listens to my prayers before I go to sleep and he took that picture with his phone. He reads me stories from the Bible. Does your deddy do that?" Crutcher glared at JJ, who continued, "It's okay if he don't. I bet my deddy would come read to you. You want me to ask him when he comes home?"

Crutcher jerked his head around toward Stephanie and spoke, "I think we're done here; this is all we need to secure his release."

The surge of relief in Jackie's heart was short-lived. She pointed to the wall and addressed Gus Crutcher, "Look at the clock. We'll never make it back in time."

In what seemed like a split second, Crutcher had retrieved his phone, punched a single number and barked an order to the person on the other end of the line, "Let me speak to Moody." And in the brief time that he waited for Moody, he turned to JJ and gave him something that almost looked like a smile. Crutcher instructed Moody, "I'm on my way back to pick up Jason Veitch. Go ahead and process him for release right away. Just have the chaplain stay with him till we get there. He's coming home tonight."

Chapter Five

Free But Not Free

J ason had only been in jail for nine days. But they were the longest days the family had known. Each member of Jason's family had something special planned for his return, but the first one they all agreed on: Dinner at the *Yes Ma'am* restaurant. They served up the best Cajun catfish and also lots of country sides like squash casserole, crunchy hush puppies, sweet turnips, and pinto beans with big slices of meat and onions. Tonight the family had the banquet room all to themselves and they were boisterous and vocal and smiling as they watched Jason eat and eat and eat. During his short time in jail, Jason had lost an alarming amount of weight and he seemed to be trying to put it all back on in one night. Jackie had already determined that tonight his dessert would be chess pie *and* banana pudding.

A waitress entered with another steaming platter of catfish filets and Larry motioned for her to place it near Jason. Jim reached over, snatching away Jason's plate and just pushed the entire platter up to Jason. The family was roaring with laughter. Stephanie shifted the platter to the table center and returned Jason's plate. JJ, who had been standing beside Jason, crawled up onto his lap. There were many stories to tell, and Jason was currently getting a colorful replay of the courageous rescue of Thumper from the villainous Vertues.

Jason, having some trouble navigating around JJ, lost a forkful of coleslaw to the floor. Jason put his hands gently on JJ's shoulders and spoke, "Here, Big Man, why don't you slide off my lap and sit on your chair?"

JJ remained on Jason's lap. Jennifer was just getting to the part of the story where she described giving Thumper his post-Vertue bath when Jason missed his plate again and a hush puppy rolled onto the table. Stephanie leaned over and half-whispered, "JJ, Honey, c'mon and get in your chair and eat your fish."

Chatting and chewing, Jason again attempted to slide JJ out of his lap, but the boy clung firmly to Jason's neck. Stephanie took JJ's chin and spoke directly to him, "JJ, your daddy can't eat his supper; now come on over and sit down in your chair."

She patted the empty chair between Jason and herself. Still, JJ did not move, and after a moment it became clear to all that Jason was having a tough time eating. Larry rose and walked around the table to JJ, "Hey, Soldier, let's move over and give your daddy some room to eat."

As Larry began to pull him away, JJ jerked away from Larry. Stephanie, seeing this uncharacteristic behavior, stood, and firmly began to pull JJ from Jason's lap. The diners grew quiet as Stephanie, Larry, and Jason tried, to no avail, to peel JJ away from his father. They were more upset than angry, as table settings began to topple in the struggle. Suddenly Hannah's voice cut through, "Leave him alone! He doesn't want to let go. He wants to hold onto his daddy. Leave him alone."

Like air seeping out of a balloon, the tension left the room. Larry and Stephanie returned to their seats. The chatter began again. The laughter returned. JJ remained in Jason's lap. And somehow they managed to eat.

JJ was drawing closer to the pirate ship. Suddenly he was upon it, and he spotted his daddy on the ship's deck at the same time Jason spotted JJ in his little boat. Jason bounded across the deck, barely missing the fists and blades of the pirates. JJ was sure if he just continued to believe, as hard as he could, that his daddy would make it safely through the mob. And then Jason, at the edge of the ship, leapt into the air and dove into the water. JJ paddled and came up to the spot where he'd last seen Jason, and there he was, popping up out of the water like a pool toy. Jason and JJ smiled, but then Jason's smile slipped easily under the water. JJ could see him, sinking lower and lower, still smiling, until the waters took him from sight. The pirates whooped and screamed. And screamed. JJ thought the screaming was the most terrible thing he had ever heard.

JJ opened his eyes and looked at his nightlight. He was at home and in his bed. But the screaming continued. He bounded off the bed and was running as soon as his bare feet hit the floor. It was only when he burst into his parents' bedroom that he realized the horrible sound was coming from his daddy. For a moment, JJ did not think it was really Jason; his eyes were too big and his face was red and distorted. And he was fighting with JJ's mom and hitting her. Paralyzed, and unable to enter or run, JJ just stared. The moment Jason laid eyes on JJ, he managed, with herculean effort, to strangle the screams down to a husky screech. Then, with Stephanie holding him fast, screams became gasps and hiccups and breathy shrieks. JJ jumped onto the bed and into his father's arms. Unable to do anything else, the three held each other in the dimness and wept.

JJ's private school building was a distinguished, aged southern lady with red brick, vines, and tall windows, all shaded by ancient live oaks. The brick winding pathways were dotted with benches and birdbaths and the occasional statue of some forgotten patron. JJ's classroom reflected the age of the institution; it was comfortable and spacious, with paneled walls and high ceilings. Counting JJ, there were an even dozen students; the school focused on individualized classes and attention. No pods or cubicles here, these rooms were warm; a place for living and learning.

Miss Inez opened the French windows to the late spring weather, then turned back to the class as she spoke, "Numbers don't have to be scary or confusing. Once you understand them, they will become friendly and useful. Who uses numbers in their job?"

Shelley raised her hand, and after Miss Inez acknowledged her, spoke up, "My mom works in a bank."

"Good, Shelley! Yes, bankers. What about you, Trey?"

Trey stood. "People that do your taxes."

"Yes, they use numbers a lot, don't they?"

JJ raised his hand and Miss Inez pointed to him. "Yes, JJ?"

"My deddy builds houses."

"Goodness, he must use numbers every day! Yes, Wyatt?"

Wyatt stood. "JJ's daddy murdered a man and now he's going to jail."

In the soundless moment that followed, a roomful of little eyes turned to the teacher.

Miss Inez gazed out at the sun-dappled lawn for a moment before speaking. "What does it mean to see through someone else's eyes?"

Trey spoke to his teacher's silhouette at the window, "Means to feel what they feel."

"Yes, to pretend that you have switched places with them and try to see things as they do." Miss Inez turned to the class and continued casually. "So, Wyatt, if you were in JJ's shoes, and someone said your daddy murdered someone, how would you feel?"

Wyatt turned directly to JJ and spoke evenly and honestly. "Sorry, JJ. I didn't mean it."

Miss Inez was smiling as she spoke, "This is good! We are learning. Now there's something else we can learn here. What do we do when we *hear* about something that happened, but we don't *know* what happened?"

Kyle offered, "Guess?"

Miss Inez laughed a little and everyone felt better as she further explained, "Hmmmmmm.... Guessing seems like a bad idea, Kyle. How many of you have heard about the problem that the Veitch family is having?" Everyone raised their hands. All but JJ. "And now, class, what do we really know? What do we *know*?"

Trey responded, "A man was killed."

"Yes, we don't know that he was murdered, just that he died."

A blond girl offered, "And JJ's daddy did it."

"Olivia, do we *know* that, or —"

"Wait!" Shelley spoke up, "No — JJ's daddy was there!"

"Yes! A man was killed. That is a *fact*. And JJ's daddy was there. That is a fact." By the look on her face, it was clear that Miss Inez was very pleased with her little people. "And what else do we know?" Seeing that her students were stumped, she nudged them a bit, "What do you *know* about JJ's daddy?"

Wyatt spoke first, "He smiles. He's nice and polite."

Then Shelley, "He helped us get our new house 'cause the bank wouldn't."

Trey spoke next, "He drove me and my brother to school when our car wasn't working."

Then JJ, "He helps me with my math homework."

Olivia offered, "My mom says he's going to be a preacher."

And finally, Shelley again, "He brought my cat home when she got lost."

Miss Inez strolled up and down the aisles as she spoke, "So JJ's dad sounds like a nice guy, doesn't he? And the things we know, or *facts,* are these: Someone was killed. JJ's dad was there. And he's a nice guy. So until we learn otherwise, how should we feel about JJ and his family? How should we treat them?"

Shelley was first again, "I feel bad for them."

"Tell JJ."

Shelley swiveled around in her desk, "I feel bad for your daddy, JJ."

Wyatt's voice was low as he spoke, "Sorry, JJ. I didn't mean to hurt your feelings."

One by one, the students spoke with a new understanding about the situation. And finally Trey asked a question of his teacher, "Miss Inez, can we say a prayer for JJ and his family?"

"Well, Trey, I think that's an excellent idea. When class is over, why don't we walk over to the chapel and say a prayer for the Veitch family? But right now, who is still scared of math?"

The students' laughter and chants of "...me, me, me..." were so loud that a couple of squirrels, descending a tree outside the window, scuttered right back up to their knothole nest. Miss Inez clutched her head in mock despair. And JJ, looking all around the room at his friends, smiled for the first time in days.

Chapter Six

A Moose and a Mountain

‹———◆———›

Jason, Stephanie, and JJ were picking at a light supper. When the doorbell rang, JJ (though he had been told not to do so) bolted and sprinted across the room, through the living room, and pulled open the front door. He froze perfectly still, mouth open, for a long moment. JJ looked up, up, up. A towering monster of a man stood in the doorway, blocking out the low afternoon sun. JJ managed a glunk sound in his throat and then cried feebly, "Deddy?" Jason entered the living room, wiping his mouth on a cloth napkin. He, too, grew very still. For the next few seconds, the only motion came from his dinner napkin, floating gently to the carpet. Jason composed himself and walked toward the door, placing the still gaping JJ firmly behind him. The big man at the door finally spoke. "I found where you live. You talk to me. I'll stand right here on the porch."

Five minutes later, the door was closed, the napkin picked up, and JJ, Jason, and Steph were seated stiffly on the living room sofa. No one spoke, but Stephanie managed to hold an uncomfortable smile on her face. The big man sat across from them on a chair that seemed to disappear beneath him. He shifted. The chair groaned. JJ spoke. "You work with my deddy?"

Without turning to her son, Stephanie warned, "JJ."

Jason spoke up, "Mr. — uh — Moose was a — I knew him when I was in jail."

JJ smiled with recognition, "What were you in jail for, Mr. Moose?"

Stephanie, without turning, "JJ."

Moose spoke in a low, flat voice, like an animated bear that JJ had seen at Six Flags. "Can I talk to your boy?"

"You can."

Moose turned to JJ. "I's in jail because I was a bully. And I thought I could hurt your daddy, too, 'cause I's bigger than him. And I tried to hurt him. But I was wrong. He's bigger than me." Moose paused for a moment and stared off into the corner. "Men turn mean in prison or they give up. Your daddy didn't do neither. What he did was read this black book all the time. I tried readin' it too after he got out. The Bible didn't make much sense until I read this one part. I learned to speak it. *If ye have faith as a grain of mustard seed, ye shall say unto this mountain, Remove hence to yonder place, and it shall remove, and nothing shall be impossible unto you.*"*

Although Moose struggled a bit to recite the passage, he cast a spell over the room. Jason asked Moose, almost tenderly, "What does that mean to you?"

Moose wiped his hands on his pants and looked up at the ceiling fan. "I think it means...you can do anything if you have a little faith. And you don't have to have a lot. Just a little bit. *Nothing will be impossible.*"** Moose looked down at JJ. "That made me feel like maybe I could change and be good, too. Like your daddy. Maybe help some kid to be good or something like that."

---

* **KJV Matthew 17:20**
** **KJV Matthew 17:20**

Stephanie was aware of being much more relaxed now and her smile was quite genuine. After a moment, she asked, "Do you have any children, Mister — Moose?"

"I do, but they don't let me see him."

"But you'd like to."

"Yes, ma'am."

Jason asked, "Where are you staying now, Moose?"

"I got a real nice trailer. And I'm gonna get some furniture for it."

"Are you working?" Stephanie asked, but immediately regretted it.

"Yes'm. I work at the Pik-A-Part out on 54. I break down the wrecked cars so they can sell the parts."

"Oh, that's nice," Stephanie said with relief. "I imagine you're good at it."

"A monkey could be good at that job." JJ sniggered at Moose's remark. "But I'm much obliged to have it. Make some money. Take care of myself. It's just...."

"You feel the need to do more," Jason finished for him.

"Yessir, I do. Used ta be I'd just spend the money fast as I'd git it. But now I...I appreciate it. And when I can save a bit, I might go to trade school or maybe set myself up in some business of my own."

Jason smiled as he spoke, "Yeah, that's the best. Do what you love, and love what you do."

"I used to think I couldn't do nuthin. I used to think I couldn't learn. But that book tells me I can do all things." For the first time, Moose smiled, revealing a missing tooth. "Not believin' never worked for me. So I'm gonna try believin'."

Jason leaned forward as he spoke, "So do you read the Bible every day now?"

"I do when the library is open."

JJ glanced up to see his parents exchange a look.

When Moose exited the Veitch home into the twilight, he was carrying Jason's Bible.

Saturday. Overcast but no rain. A breezy, warm day in early summer. It was a perfect day for walking, and JJ and the girls had trekked to the drugstore, which had bins of self-serve candy. Picking out, measuring, and matching the candy was almost as good as eating it. Almost. As they strolled the sidewalks toward home, each carried a small, white bag with pink bunting printed on it. Approaching a familiar looking side street, an old automobile skeleton heralded this as the road to the Vertue house. As always, they skirted the area, but this time it was too late. Three figures began to move in on them and one was Travis Vertue. Travis and his two gangsters quickly surrounded JJ and his cousins. Travis wiped his nose on his sleeve and narrowed his pale pig eyes. Then he spoke, "You took my dog."

Hannah fired back, "The fact of the matter is, you took *my* dog."

"Witch, you took my dog!"

One of the gang echoed menacingly, "....took his dog..."

Travis moved in on Hannah. "Think you can come on my propaty and take what you want?"

Another echo, "...come on his property..."

"What if I come to your house, huh?"

"...come to your house, *yeah*...."

Anna Grace shielded Patience as Travis and his demented chorus continued their rant, "Take something from you!"

"...something from you..."

JJ didn't like Travis' close proximity to Hannah and spoke as firmly as he could, "You better just leave us alone."

"And I know who you are, too. Your daddy's a jailbird."

"...jailbird, *yeah*...."

Travis stuck a dirty finger in JJ's face and raised his voice, "Yer daddy thinks he can go 'round killing people but he got caught, din't he?"

"...got caught..."

"And now they gonna lock him up for good!"

"...lock up the jailbird..."

Abruptly, Patience spoke up, "He's not a jailbird, he's my Uncle Bird!"

Travis glared at the little girl, "There ya go; even his name says it. Bird. Jail-Bird!"

JJ dashed over and placed his arm protectively around Patience, attempting to herd the girls away. "C'mon, let's go home." In an instant, one of the boys pushed Hannah to the sidewalk and Travis grabbed the bag from JJ and began to beat him with it. Although the weapon was only a bag of candy, the assault was shockingly vicious, and JJ was pummeled to the ground with non-stop whips of the shredding bag, candy flying like bullets in all directions. Hannah screamed with as much force as she could muster, "Stop it stop it stop it right now!"

A passing car slowed, the driver eyed the situation. Travis dropped the bag before speaking low, "This is just a little reminder of what's comin'. You all think you better'n me. You'll find out."

"...find out, *yeah...*"

Travis turned his gaze to the girls, "And you gonna pay for takin' my dog."

"...pay for it..."

Standing over JJ's little figure, he looked down and grinned, "You too, jailbird."

"...you too..."

The three boys drifted, like specters, into an overgrown lot. The car moved on. The girls were still and looked like they were feeling sick. JJ continued to lay on the ground, streaks of colorful candy bleeding down his face.

Night. Almost bedtime. Hannah was lounging upon her quilted comforter, reading, while her sisters sat upon the lower tier of their bunk beds. Anna Grace was industriously styling Pay-Pay's hair, while Patience busied herself switching heads on doll bodies. Jennifer leaned into the room and addressed her girls, "Has anyone seen my gold star earrings?"

"Thumper's wearing them," offered Hannah.

Jennifer turned slowly to her middle daughter. "Anna Grace?"

"He looked so shiny after his bath, I thought he should get dressed up."

"I'm not even gonna ask about my missing panty hose, then." Jennifer watched her girls for a moment before walking over and joining

Hannah on her bed. "How would you girls like to spend a night or two with Gommi next week?"

Hannah put her book aside. "You and daddy going somewhere?"

"No. In fact, I might just go to Gommi's with you."

Anna Grace's eyes lit up. "A slumber party?"

"A little bit like a slumber party. And we're going to ask JJ, too."

As she tried to fit an Elmo head onto a Betsy Wetsy doll, Patience declared sagely, "Boy's can't go to slumber parties." Elmo didn't fit. She searched for another head.

Anna Grace, as the older sister, corrected Patience with, "Sure they can. They just have to wear different pajamas and can't hear our secrets."

Hannah eyed her mother levelly. "What's up, Mom?"

Jennifer waited until both Anna Grace and Patience had joined them on the bed before speaking. "Well, JJ's parents need some time alone, and your grandmother does *not* need to be alone, because she is feeling very sad —"

"About Uncle Bird?"

"Yes, Anna Grace, about Uncle Bird, and —"

"Jail?"

"Yes. Jail."

"But Uncle Bird got out of jail," Patience protested.

"Yes. Yes, he did. For a while."

Jennifer looked at her girls. In most ways they were typical little girls. But sometimes they exhibited intuition and humanity that was not learned; it could only be God-given. Patience crawled into her lap, and Jennifer continued, "But some people think he did something wrong and must pay for it. And he has to talk to those people. And he, and your Aunt Stephanie....."

Across town, JJ's parents were having a very similar conversation with JJ. "....have a big decision to make," continued Jason. "See, JJ, because a man died, even though it was an accident, there are people who want to be absolutely sure that I didn't mean to...harm him."

Stephanie picked up the thread of thought, "And they have given us a choice. If we decide to take their offer, and say that it was Daddy's fault, but it was an accident, then he will go to jail. For three years."

"Don't do it! Deddy, don't!"

Stephanie placed a calming hand on her son's tiny shoulder. "But, JJ, if he takes the other choice — and this other choice is called a *trial* —"

"— then one of two things will happen. They might let me come right back home and stay home always. Or they might make me go to jail...for...for a long time."

"For a long, long time?"

"For thirty years."

There it was. Out in the open. Jason was suddenly aware he had never spoken these details out loud. His heart was pounding. He and Stephanie watched JJ carefully, ready for anything. After a moment, JJ spoke solemnly. "It's a big decision."

A grin came to Stephanie's face. Her son never failed to amaze her. "Yes, it is a big decision," she began, "but it's not your decision. We don't want you worrying about it. Okay? We just wanted you to know."

"Now," Jason announced, "it's bedtime for all the munchkins in this house!"

Stephanie helped JJ to snuggle under the covers as Jason sat on the edge of the bed and pulled the ribbon that kept their place in JJ's Bible. "When last we left our heroes," Jason began dramatically, "we were in the book of Psalms. Remember what psalms means?"

"Songs!"

"Right, songs! And —"

"Deddy?"

"Yes."

"Read to me about the flood."

"You want to hear about Noah?"

"Yes."

"Are you sure you want to hear about scary stuff right before bedtime? There's rain and a terrible flood. And days and days of awful darkness."

"Yes."

"Why, Honey?"

"Because after the flood, there was a rainbow."

And so it came to pass that all the children were carted off to Gommi Jackie and Poppi Larry's house. Jennifer had joined them, to help wrangle the kids. They had no idea how long the visit would last, but all agreed that Jackie needed the distraction of family and company. Jason and Stephanie now had some much-needed alone time. They needed this time to pray, think, discuss; for as JJ had put it, "It's a big decision."

It was well after ten pm at the grandparents' house, and only Jackie and JJ were awake. The girls were fast asleep on Gommi's big four-poster bed, and Jennifer had retired to the guest bedroom some time earlier. Jackie's bed was strewn with empty paper plates, with Thumper and Bojangles lazily licking a paper plate that had strayed to the floor. JJ placed his plate, with a few sugary cake morsels remaining, on the floor, and the pups made a beeline for it. JJ, sitting on the bed with his legs crossed, was watching his grandmother. Jackie's face was turned toward the children's movie that played silently on the TV; a plate with uneaten cake rested in her hand. JJ wanted to ask his grandmother why her face was getting skinny, but something told him that would be a bad idea. Lately she acted like someone does when they are sick. JJ eyed the sleeping girls, Gommi, the dogs, Gommi's cake, then the dogs again. "Gommi, don't you like your cake?"

"Huh? No, Sweetie, do you want it?"

"No, ma'am."

"Ready for seepy?"

"Hannah said that you are sad. About Deddy."

"Don't you worry about that. That's a big person problem."

"Gommi, can I ask you a question?"

Jackie placed her cake carefully onto the bed and pushed some stray hairs off her forehead. She hadn't had her hair done in...how long? What else was she neglecting? She smiled at the little man beside her. "Of course you can. What is it that you want to ask me?"

"Does Deddy have a bully?"

Jackie stirred, becoming more alert. After a moment, she began to speak carefully. "I never thought of it that way, but I guess you're right. The people who are...making it hard for your daddy...have a lot of power. And they are using your daddy to get something they want. And it don't appear that they care whether they hurt him or not. So, I guess that's what a bully is: somebody who pushes somebody else around, just because they can." Jackie watched JJ carefully. He seemed to be troubled; deep in thought. "JJ. What made you ask me about bullies?" No response. "Honey, you know you can talk to me about anything."

"Gommi, how can you stop a bully?"

Jackie reached over and absently pushed a wet nose away from the bed and moved her cake out of dog danger. "Whew! That's a big question. That's a grownup question, and I'm trying to figure it out right now myself. But one thing's for sure. The bully is wrong. The person being picked on should never feel bad or...or ashamed because they are being bullied. You — they — are good. They're fine. They're great. The bully is the one that's wrong."

"So how do you make them stop hurting you?"

"Don't know but maybe we can figure it out! I never thought about your daddy having a bully. But now that you've helped me see...there are a lot of books written on how to handle bullies. We can order some, okay? And the Bible talks about bullies."

"Really?"

"The Bible says when someone hits you, you should turn the other cheek. That means, don't fight back; if they hit you on one cheek, offer them the other cheek to hit. And it says...it says...an eye for an eye... which means, if they hit you, you should hit them back, and..."

Jackie and JJ sat silent, totally bewildered. The one book that they trusted the most, had just laid a contradiction before them. Suddenly Jackie came to attention with a jerk that was big enough to derail another attempt at cake theft by Thumper. "JJ, I think I've got it! The Bible gives you lots of ideas and lots of choices. So that must mean one choice is right sometime and another choice is right another time!"

"So sometimes you turn your cheek and sometimes you punch them in the eye?"

Jackie was feeling a tingling of life within her body that had been long missing. Her eyes were alert. "JJ, I think I just figured something out! And it's all because of you. The Bible gives us lots of rules and choices and lessons, doesn't it? But it never tells us exactly what to do. If it gave us the exact answer to every question, then we wouldn't have to think. And I think God wants us to think! And to learn. And to choose; to make the right choices on our own!"

"But Gommi, how do we know which choice is the right one?"

"I think we would....we should say our prayers and ask for help. And we listen to what we hear when it's quiet. Listen. And then, we should feel peace. After we act, we should feel peace if we made the right choice. And if we don't feel peace, then we learn a lesson for next time. And when we stand and fight, we know we're right if that fight brings us peace. It's not easy..."

"Sometimes we walk away and sometimes we fight."

Jackie added, "And if we've done the right thing, I think we feel good and clean, like after a storm."

"Good and clean, like when the sun comes out after the rain. And makes a rainbow."

Anna Grace awoke with a snort, and spoke groggily. "Raining? Is it raining?" JJ and Jackie were doing their best to keep straight faces. But it was hard with Anna Grace sitting so grandly and imperiously on the bed. Cake frosting had neatly glued a paper plate to the side of her face.

Chapter Seven

That Summer

Stephanie had decided that the house was too empty without JJ. She was fully aware that she and Jason had to make the biggest decision of their lifetimes, a decision that would affect the remainder of their lives. Privacy and solitude might help. However, the fact was, she wanted JJ back home with them. She wanted as much normalcy as possible and life could not be normal without her son. But this was Jason's choice, so she would not complain. He wanted the two of them to have some time to seriously consider their options, and the potential consequences of their actions.

Both Jason and Steph had spoken to every adult member of the family, and they all seemed as baffled by the law — the wording of the law and the consequences of the law — as they were. Although they had yet to meet their attorney Mr. Kam in person, Jason had called him up and asked him point blank, "Should I take the plea bargain and go to jail for three years, or roll the dice with a jury trial?"

Mr. Kam spoke without hesitation, "Jason, if you take the jury trial, there's no middle ground. You'll be exonerated completely or you will go to jail for thirty years. Taking a jury trial will be the worst mistake of your life. There's no way any twelve jurors are going to think and vote the same way on every detail. Take the plea bargain."

So Jason had his answer from the man they had hired to provide answers. Kam had been involved in countless trials and his advice was backed by experience.

But one thing was missing: Mr. Kam had never been to jail. Jason had no doubt that God had directly saved him while he was behind bars. He had even been led to bring one of his potential attackers to know Christ! But the fear; the constant, gnawing fear that ate at him fed hungrily on his weak, human side. Though Jason saw miracles, he was also subjected to constant noise, no space, no privacy, no dignity; to cold and grime and stink and claustrophobia. And worst of all, he was robbed of time with his family. Mr. Kam was telling him to serve the three years, but strong as Jason's faith was, he was afraid his fragile human side was not equipped to survive three years of that horror. Cornered.

And these were the things that Jason had told Stephanie. Stephanie had only nodded, because she felt the same. She heard the conflicting information. She felt the rage building up inside of her. She, too, felt the suffocating, maddening grip of suddenly realizing there was no way out. If only they could go apologize to someone or show them a video of what really happened or just talk to a judge, and then he would see they were just ordinary people and Jason was not a killer!

Jason had always felt a great deal of respect and awe for police officers; they put their lives on the line each day. In fact, he idolized them a bit. And they were trained on handling situations just like Jason was facing. That night last February he was only doing, with complete confidence, what the officer had told him. When the battered van approached his site, lights off, he prayed they would just keep going. But instead they pulled right into the driveway of a half-built two-story. What legitimate reason could they possibly have for being there at midnight? Time passed and he could not tell what was happening in the dark. He imagined he would have seen an interior light come on if the intruders had exited the van, but what if there was no interior light?! Just to be safe, he called 911. And waited. And called 911 again. And waited. He called Stephanie's dad, Billy, just to catch him up on what was happening. And then, alone in the dark, flat on the cold ground in the woods on his own property, he waited for the police.

At long last, Jason saw car lights approaching. They pulled into the driveway right behind the van, and Jason pulled his stiff bones up from the frosty ground and began to move toward the two vehicles. And then he saw it: It wasn't the police. It was Billy! Billy was knocking on the side of the van. Billy could be dead before Jason even reached him! Jason fired a shot into the air and ran to the van, shouting, "Get out of the vehicle! You are trespassing on my private property and the police are on their way. Get out of the vehicle now!"

Momentarily, two figures slid out of the front seat and stood beside the van. They were both speaking Spanish non-stop, and Jason could not make anything out. He told them to get on the ground and Billy demonstrated with gestures. Finally, both men were on the ground with hands behind their backs and all was quiet. From within the back of the van came a dull thump and the vehicle rocked slightly on its tires. There were more inside! The next few minutes were sheer madness, out there in the dark and cold with shouting and confusion and no police car, Dear Lord, no police! The earlier warning gunshot — Jason's first — had started an adrenaline rush that was disorienting. And when a third man finally jumped out of the van, he was combative, yelling and lunging at Jason and Billy. Then there was a scuffle and they were slipping on the icy ground and despite being told to stay on the ground, the third man got up and lurched at Jason and there was another gunshot.....

It would seem this was a clear cut case of standing your ground and protecting home and property. It was no secret that Jason had been robbed repeatedly and he had reported it to the police and the insurance company. Jason wasn't the only one being robbed of copper. And there was no doubt that these men were intruding on private property in the middle of the night. What right or reason did they have to be there, and at such an outrageous hour? But this situation had turned into something of a *cause celebre.* Everyone involved seemed to have an agenda. The newscasters labeled Jason a racist, simply because the dead man was Hispanic. In her church group, a lifelong friend of Jackie's got up and moved away from her in Sunday School, proclaiming she didn't want to sit next to a murderer's mother. Because the family was fairly well-to-do, reporters turned it into a "privileged rich" case. And a career politician was determined to use this case to garner the poor and Black and Hispanic vote by putting this "rich, entitled, racist" into jail for life.

It seemed there was no anchor, no sanity. Everything that Jason and Steph had believed in was gone, as if the very ground beneath them had disappeared. Jackie told them to make the decision that would bring them peace. *But what decision would bring them peace?* With JJ gone, they had discussed until they were both exhausted and seemed no closer to peace; to a solution. Still, they plowed on and prayed.

One night, Jason and Stephanie sat on the living room sofa and stared out the picture window at the full moon. There didn't seem to be anything to say. Words weren't helping. Finally, Jason roused himself and spoke, "Steph, I want to propose something to you. And I don't think you'll like it. But I feel very strongly about it and I have to speak."

Her heart pounding, Stephanie turned toward her husband and steeled herself, vowing not to show any emotion that would add to his troubles. As evenly as possible, she said, "Go ahead Jason. Say whatever you need to say."

"Steph, I know you feel it's important for us to have quiet and space to work this out, but....but I...but I just miss JJ."

"I miss him, too!"

"It just feels incomplete without him. And too quiet! And when I, if I have to go away, I would regret every second that I spent without him."

"Jason, I thought you wanted him to stay with Jackie."

"I don't remember who wanted it or why, but I want him home; I want him home now!"

Tears of relief flooded Stephanie's face as she hugged Jason and cried, "Me too! Me too!"

A little while later, both Jason and Stephanie felt a bit better for crying. Or perhaps the effort it took to cry used up their last bit of energy. They sat, completely still, in each other's arms, not wanting to move, ever. Finally Jason spoke. "Steph. It's all just too big for me. Too confusing. I feel like my brain doesn't work anymore. I don't see a way out of this."

"Jason, don't you believe that God knows what to do?"

"Yes, I do, Steph. I really do. I just wish He'd let me in on it."

JJ's feet left the sidewalk. Travis was lifting him by his shirt. When Travis tossed him, JJ's legs buckled the moment they hit the hard concrete. Before JJ could get his bearings, Travis positioned himself on JJ's chest. He slapped JJ's face over and over, then got up as if to walk away. When JJ managed to get to his feet, Travis wheeled and grabbed him by the neck, jerking him about wildly. Travis' gang urged him on, shouting suggestions, and taunting JJ by chanting, "...killer, killer, killer!"

One big swing and Travis lost his grip on JJ's neck, sending the smaller boy sprawling off the sidewalk and onto a storm drain. JJ quickly gained his footing and ran for his life. Apparently satisfied, the hulking boys did not chase him, but continued to taunt him. JJ could hear their cries and insults until the blood pumping in his ears drowned them out.

By the time JJ made it home, he had also managed to hide some of the damage. He'd tucked in his shirt, run his fingers through his hair, and with spit and some leaves, got off most of the dirt and blood. He just wanted to sit here on his front porch where he would be safe. He wanted to sit here until it got dark, so maybe his parents wouldn't know what was happening to him. He was so ashamed. He wanted to hide.

JJ looked up to see a strange car pull into the drive. It was old and beat up. It was Moose's car. Too late to hide, JJ just ducked his head as Moose, Bible in hand, lumbered through the blinding summer sun toward the porch. But instead of going inside, Moose sat down and looked over at the dirt in JJ's hair and the finger marks on his neck.

They sat for a moment in silence and then JJ realized it would be rude to ignore Mr. Moose.

"You here to read the Bible with my deddy?

"Yeah."

"That's my deddy's Bible you got."

"He give it to me. To keep."

"I know he did."

"How'd you get them marks on your neck?"

JJ pulled a long blade of grass and began to study it.

Moose spoke up again, "When I's a kid, I got picked on, too."

"How come?"

"'Cause my name."

"Moose?"

"'Cause my real name."

"What's your real name?"

"Lois."

"Why'd you get named Lois?"

"I think my mama was gonna call me Louis, but she didn't spell it right."

"Didn't your mama ever learn to spell?"

"I dunno. Folks raised me didn't tell me much about her."

"Did the folks that raised you call you Lois?"

"They called me Lou, but Lois was still wrote down as my name someplace. Some teacher got ahold of it and told some kids. So I got picked on."

"Moose?"

"Huh?"

"When they picked on you, what did you do?

"The wrong things."

"What's the right thing?"

"Dunno. Trying to find out."

And with that, Moose got up and went inside.

In the deep south, there is no autumn. Instead, there's a slow dying of the summer. Images of hills painted gold and red are just for those who live up north, to be enjoyed by southerners only on television and postcards. Evergreens cover most of the southern states and as the hardwoods quietly fall into withered slumber, the green landscape remains. The brisk October days enjoyed by residents from Kentucky to Maine are not known in the lower states. The overpowering heat of a Georgia summer just eases into something slightly more bearable, and rains no longer turn to steam upon hitting the pavement. Summer in the south fights to hang on until the bitterness of January finally overtakes it.

If asked back in March if he could survive one more day of this terror, of this not-knowing, Jason surely would have said no. And yet he did. And so did Jackie and Stephanie and all the family and their friends. When Jackie first got the news, she was certain it would all be cleared up within minutes. For the most part, this same hope was still keeping Jason and his family sane. "Any minute now, they'll drop the charges." "Any minute now, I'll wake up."

But day gave way to night, which bled into another sunrise and on and on. And they managed to shop and eat and pray and work and clean and even appear at times to be a normal family. They managed to put one foot in front of the other. But rarely did they congratulate themselves for surviving so far (what was it now? five months; seven months?) because if they looked at the time they had survived they might have to admit that this could go on for another month, or seven months or..... No, it was too much to bear to think this would go on much longer. Human beings were not meant to function under this type of stress. No, this would all be gone from their lives, soon. Tomorrow. Yes, probably tomorrow.

Brother Jim continued to preach his sermons every Sunday morning. He was acutely aware that this arrest of his brother and the publicity and trial which followed had thrust his family into the spotlight. Often at times like these, the most innocent remark can be misconstrued, and here he was speaking to crowds several times per week! He had to re-evaluate. He had to be careful. His church members were remarkably restrained when it came to bringing up the current family situation, but he had to be on guard.

Jim knew that he could not turn his pulpit into a political venue. But in looking for inspiration for his sermons, he found that almost any subject could relate to his family's trials. It seemed that everyone had to cope with judgment and being judged, self-doubt, lack of faith, fear, loss, and most importantly, how to be a spiritual being living in a human body. Though our faith may be strong, our poor human bodies and minds often pull focus and demand our attention. One might even say that living on faith sounds easy, until there's no money to feed your children. And so these issues came into sharp focus for Jim as he prepared his sermons.

Also, each Sunday seemed to find new faces at service. These were mysterious strangers who sat in the back, did not welcome being recognized, and rarely attended again. Jim suddenly realized, first-hand, a small fraction of what his little brother must be feeling every day. Jason was being watched, scrutinized, judged. Jim wished he could protect Jason like he did when they were kids. He wondered how this constant awareness of being in the spotlight was wearing on Jason. Constantly being judged and criticized can make you wary of even your closest friends. Suspicion can turn into paranoia, and paranoia can lead you away from yourself.

Jennifer wanted the girls to have the sanest, safest upbringing she could give them. She wished they could be left totally out of this nightmare But, like it or not, her daughters were in the midst of it. Jennifer had learned to filter everything that she did and said in order to protect the girls. What was happening was not hidden though, as she and Jim thoughtfully and carefully explained details of the family's unfortunate situation. But she was terribly concerned that some casual remark or comment might be misunderstood by the girls. She was cautious about every word she spoke. Even phone conversations became difficult, lest some response was misconstrued and troubled the girls. But this led to another problem: How and when should she and her husband discuss the terribly important issues that were now a part of their lives? The girls were at home most of the time. It did occur to Jennifer that she was more grateful than ever that the girls were home-schooled and protected from the cruelty that dwells in some children. But they were not completely cut off from interaction with others. There was church and Sunday School and Sunbeams. There was the evening news and newspapers. And she was well aware that every child who interacted with the girls had been told some version of what happened with their Uncle Bird.

Jennifer became vaguely aware that she and her family were being forced to reinvent themselves; to restructure their lives. As time wore on and the trial date loomed in the nebulous future, she was disgusted that the entire family was forbidden to speak of the incident to anyone at any time. She had to arm the girls with certain responses in case they were challenged. And the local television stations seemed intent upon painting a portrait of Jason as a madman; racist and smug with his wealthy lifestyle. It was insanity! The reporters could say anything they wanted! The police and witnesses and family member of the deceased man could say anything, yet Jason and his family were allowed to say nothing!

Jennifer was also aware that her mother-in-law had become distressed thinking about the mother of the man who was killed. Jackie desperately wanted to speak with her, attempt to comfort her; just reach out. But she was forbidden. This only added to the burdens. Jennifer carried her own burdens through the summer and fall and winter of 2008, reinventing herself as mother and protector and teacher.

Though it was not obvious at first, Jackie had become obsessed. A woman of strong faith, she had always found her answers within her faith, her friends, her Bible. Now she was disoriented. Her child had been taken from her under the most unexpected and absurd circumstances and the mama tiger was released within her. And yet, no matter how much she prayed, or how faithfully she searched her Bible, the situation grew worse and worse. Days dragged into weeks and this terrible incident and the publicity and the upcoming trial became an obsession.

At some point, something had snapped within her and she felt betrayed. God had placed within Jackie the protective instincts of a mother, yet seemed to have perversely taken away any ability to help her child. And why wasn't God showing her the way?! In one terrifying moment, she suddenly thought of the passage, *For God so loved the world, that He gave his only begotten son....* * Was this it? Was this what God was asking her to do? Was this the test of faith He was asking? And what about Abraham when God told him to sacrifice Isaac? Was God asking her to sacrifice her own son? Because if she stood by and did nothing, wasn't she sacrificing Jason? No! This was too much. This wasn't part of the deal. It should never be asked of a human being to prove their love to their Heavenly Father by sacrificing their child. And if she did not save him, if she did not do everything within her power to rescue him, she was surely sacrificing him! She had done everything that she thought her faith had led her to do. She had prayed, read, bargained, cried, stopped eating and sleeping. What was she supposed to do now?

And when it seemed that God had abandoned her, she confronted Him. She told Him she did not have the strength to sacrifice her son. And if He wouldn't do anything, then she would. If God wouldn't do anything, then she would do something! Yes, she would.

This was the start of the obsession that drove Jackie to the brink of death. She decided to educate herself as a lawyer, juror, lawmaker, judge, and more if necessary. She would find the law, the rule, the hidden clue that would save Jason. She began to buy stacks of books, tracked down and confronted lawyers, and endlessly pored over her computer. She knew she could find it. She knew she would find the way to free Jason. She just needed to look in the right book.

Larry knew better than to try to stop Jackie when she had her mind set. Initially, he had helped her by picking up books and assisting her with the intricacies of the internet. When she began to forgo food, he brought her juice and vitamins and stood by while she drank it. He

---

* **KJV John 3:16**

65

made sure she went to bed when he did, although often he woke up to find the bed empty, or to see her just sitting, staring into the darkness.

Then things began to move in a dangerous direction. There were mysterious scrapes and dings on the car. Jackie's face was clearly showing the ravages of stress and malnutrition. Larry went to the office every day and came home each evening to wild tales of conspiracy and dark forces. He wanted to help, but how? So he just continued to listen to her, bring her juice, and try to help her. Larry didn't even realize that what he was giving, his support and stability, was what she needed most.

When Jason was first released from prison, he was lifted by euphoria. He could see nothing ahead, for he was overwhelmed with the joy of freedom and return to his family. But the days wore on and life called him. There was the matter of work. He and Stephanie had a little saved, but it would not last long. Going back to work; back to the very site where this terrible thing had happened did not seem an option. But indeed it was the only option. Who would hire him now?

Jason began to experience panic attacks when he left the house. He made it to the truck, but couldn't seem to remember what to do next. Instead of turning the key in the ignition, he sat perfectly still, as if refusing to move would keep him safe. On one particular morning, he panicked so badly that he needed to get back in the house to tell Stephanie to call the doctor. But he couldn't go back to the house; it seemed so far away. So he just sat still, trying not to move, trying to be small. As in prison, he felt that if he was silent and small and still enough, he wouldn't get hurt anymore.

On the first day back on the site, Jason did find some comfort. Perhaps it was being back in the familiar routine, or maybe it was just the victory of making it to the site and getting out of the truck. The TV reporters had painted Jason as an all-out racist and it seemed that had cost him some of his workers. And yet many more had remained; and some of these were Hispanic. When he told Stephanie about the loyalty of his remaining Hispanic crew, she cried. And when he told her that some of them had been working without pay, waiting for Jason to get on his feet and write the checks, they both cried.

Though it seemed impossible, Jason managed to work. There were no more copper thefts, though Jason wasn't sure about the reason for this. He was just grateful to be making some progress.

Then came the day that JJ's little dog became ill. She was gasping for breath and Jason didn't know if she would make it to the vet. Halfway there, sirens and lights pulled Jason to the side of the road. In his desperation to save the pup, he had been driving slightly over the speed limit. When the officer approached his vehicle, Jason suddenly felt as if a hammer had hit him in the chest. This was it! They would run his plates and find out he was a killer and put him back in jail. And who would get the dog to the vet? And who would raise JJ? After the officer drove away, Jason's hands shook so hard that he could barely start the engine.

The nights were the worst. Whatever Jason managed to keep hidden exploded when his brain should have been resting. His sleep seemed shallow and the slightest noise woke him up, and often he could not tell the difference between reality and dreams. The worst dreams had to do with Juan Carlos Reymundo. One night he dreamed that the painting which hung over their bed, a soothing scene that both he and Stephanie loved, had been replaced with a photo of Juan Carlos lying on a metal coroner's slab. After a moment, the photograph of Juan Carlos opened its dead eyes. Another night, he was in the middle of a dream so horrible that he awakened Stephanie with his screaming. As she held him in her arms and tried to calm him, Jason glanced over to see Juan Carlos leering at him from their closet.

Stephanie was lost. As Jackie often thought, Stephanie too wondered how this could have happened to them. Sure, you heard about things like this, and you always thought it happened to a certain type of person. Jason was a hard-working man who was studying to become a pastor. He had never, in his life, knowingly broken any law. Jason was the type of guy who drove 53 in a 55 mile zone. He paid every bill on the day it arrived. He was gentle and peaceful and did his best to abide by God's law as well as man's law. So what, what had happened? And if this could happen to Jason, who was safe? Even this horrible loss of life had only occurred because Jason was obeying an officer of the law!

But Stephanie kept this all to herself. She simply wanted to be there for her family; to make sure she was there to listen to and support Jason and make certain to protect JJ as best she could.

If she felt overwhelmed, she revealed it only to her daddy. Stephanie's dad Billy was a quiet, solitary man who treasured his privacy. Stephanie often thought he would have been happiest if born into a time when there were no phones or television sets, and everyone grew their own food. He had often talked about building a little cabin in the woods and living on trout and corn that he raised himself. And though she didn't want to burden him, she knew that being with her dad was the only place where she could be herself. Having been a witness to the shooting had no doubt damaged Billy. At the same time, he alone was able to offer his daughter a clear first-hand report of what had happened on that night in February. Like the other members of her family, Stephanie managed to get through the summer by putting one foot in front of the other. As Jim often said, "Do your best and let God do the rest."

Finally, the Georgia summer of 2008 began to wear itself out.

Chapter Eight

A Hard Fall - A Dark Winter

T he Carpenter's home was filled with the smell of cooking, and Larry was delighted that Jackie had agreed to a small dinner party. The kitchen windows were open to the outside, and a fresh autumn breeze kept the house at a comfortable temperature. The living room, which had been transformed into Jackie's command center, was still stacked with mountains of books and the walls were plastered with newspaper and magazine articles and countless sticky notes. Jackie had spent months researching the law, court cases, and contacting everyone who might help Jason. But she had agreed to leave it all behind for just one night, so the living room lights were turned off. They would cook in the kitchen, eat in the dining room, then retire to the den. Larry had made certain that one of Jackie's best and most level-headed friends was invited, and he was talking to Fontella in hushed tones as she stirred pots and checked on the meal. Larry moved out of Fontella's path as she opened the oven door, and he spoke to her quietly, "She's on that computer day and night and going through every law book she can find."

Fontella delicately blotted her forehead with a handkerchief and replied in her exquisitely melodic voice, "Lord, Lord help my Jackie."

"We got the best lawyer money can buy, but Jackie thinks she alone is gonna find the secret that will free Jason."

"Did you get the lawyer you were trying to get?"

"Yeah, I think he's a Chinese guy. Mr. Kam. He's supposed to be the best."

"Jim told me that the police had to bring her home one night!"

"Fontella, the officer said she knew she was supposed to go to Cochran Mill, but didn't know where she was or how to get there!"

"Larry, is she always so forgetful now?"

"Not always. Sometimes she goes off on an idea and there's no stopping her. It's like she's possessed. Fontella, did you know she hand-wrote a letter to that defense attorney Evelyn Pitt and begged her, as a woman, to drop the charges?"

Fontella gasped in disbelief as Larry continued, "And she did this after we had been warned not to talk about the case with anyone. Kam called her up and came down on her hard."

Fontella wiped imaginary spots off the spotless stove top, then asked, "But is that really so bad? It seems like something any mother might do for her son."

"Fontella, Kam told her if they wanted to use it against her, it could actually sway the jury against Jason. Yes, what she did was really that bad. And I never know what she might do next...."

Fontella's forehead creased in worry. "We got to find a way to turn her around."

"I'm trying all I know —"

Jackie exploded into the kitchen, chattering non-stop. Her energy was high and her speech chirpy, but her clothes hung loosely on a skeletal frame and her eyes darted erratically. Speaking rapidly, she sometimes slurred her words together. "Larry, that computer in the living room is running real slow every time I go to search for anything on a government site or police it just slows down to a crawl did you know Fontella brought over a meatloaf and some Parker House Rolls and stuff I told her I had everything all planned out but that was nice anyway let me just check on the beans and then I want you to look at that computer Honey would you look at the laptop it's running real slow and —"

At the sound of the front doorbell Jackie abruptly dashed from the room. She pulled open the door and greeted Jason and Steph and JJ with a big smile. Lurching forward, Jackie grabbed Jason and held him tightly, sobbing convulsively. Stephanie and a bewildered JJ watched the weird display in silence. Fontella entered. After some uncomfortable moments, Jason attempted to peel himself away from his mother. He asked with genuine concern, "Mom. Hey, Mom. What'sa matter?"

Jackie appeared to be completely lost as to why Jason would ask such a question and laughingly replied, "Nothing; nothing's wrong. Why would you think something's wrong?"

Fontella ushered Steph and JJ inside and closed the front door behind them, saying, "Hey, we better get those coats off before you get too hot!"

Jackie snapped, "I know that! I know it's too dark for coats!"

Leaning in, Jackie spoke confidentially to Jason. "Jason, will you come look at this computer in the living room? Whenever I get on a — whenever I look for anything official, they slow it down. They don't want me to get in there or something."

Larry had joined them and suggested, "Honey, why don't you just settle —"

"Why don't you just stay out of it?!"

Fontella spoke gently, "I think he just means —"

"I *know* what he means." Jackie hissed. "He means just let it go, just lay down and give up like the rest of you, just let 'em come on in and lock up Jason without a fight. You all just sit back and — somebody's got to do something! You all want Jason to go to jail and just sit and rot with those —"

The sound of JJ's crying stopped Jackie cold. She looked at him blankly for a couple of seconds before saying, "I need to check on the... don't wanna let the rolls burn..."

Jackie walked toward the kitchen, but stopped in the doorway, hesitated uncertainly, then turned the other direction and disappeared down the hallway.

In the quiet that followed, Fontella smiled and offered, "I'll just go check on the din —"

The first of several crashes pulled the family into the darkened living room. Larry hit the lights. Standing mid-room, Jackie was holding the shattered remains of a laptop. She appeared to have struck the laptop repeatedly on the corner of a heavy table, as the marble top was covered with bits of the shattered screen. Jackie looked at her family and began to explain, "It was running slow, you know, real slow..."

The remains of the laptop fell from her hands, revealing bloody palms. In slow motion, Jackie crumpled to the floor.

Jackie didn't know any of the people at the party. She felt compelled to sneak out and search for her boys. Both Jim and Jason had been missing for some time. The worst part was that no one believed her. Every time she told someone — even Stephanie or Jennifer — they just smiled or laughed politely as if she had told a little joke. It wasn't a joke! Her boys were missing and no one seemed to know or care. But maybe....just maybe she was supposed to act as if it were a joke! Ah, yes, that would explain everything! That would explain why everyone acted as if they were dismissing her concerns. They were all being watched! They were being spied on and monitored and if they let on that they were searching for the boys...suddenly she understood. She wanted to tell someone — someone she trusted — that she was on to the game. She got it. She would be quiet from now on. She wouldn't make a scene, in fact, she wouldn't even let anyone know she was still searching. She had been warned not to talk to anyone, but she could still do something.

A woman in a white dress and cap handed her a cup of tea, but she refused it. The woman was insistent and said, "Tea is more important than you know. We're monitoring the tea for you."

Suddenly it was time for her to speak to the group. Jackie wished she had worn something more appropriate; the guests were in evening clothes and she was wearing an old nightgown. But no one else seemed to be bothered by it. As she took the stage, the room grew quiet and everyone turned to her. For what reason? What was she supposed to say? Why were they looking to her for direction? Surely she was more confused than anyone at this terrible party. She felt so weak; just wanted to sit down. Before she knew it, the crowd was applauding and she was leaving the stage, grateful that the speech was over. Strangely, she could not recall a single word she'd said.

Making her way through the crowd, Jackie tried to remember what she was supposed to do now. Her eyelids were so heavy that they kept shutting. She needed to find someone....her boys! She needed to find her sons, but now she also knew she had to be quiet about it; she was forbidden to say a word to anyone.

A tall Chinese gentleman walked directly to Jackie. He was wearing a tuxedo and carrying a silver tray. The man bowed and proffered the tray; Jackie took an envelope from it. As the man turned to leave, she asked, "What's this?"

He didn't look at Jackie, but glanced at the envelope in her hand, and simply said, "Remember, you're not allowed to open it yet."

The Chinese man looked right into her eyes and back to the envelope. Jackie followed his eyes to the white envelope and realized there was a single word printed on it: Vertue. "What could that mean?" she wondered out loud, and then looked back to the paper a second time. Now the word on the envelope was Verdict. Oh, how she wanted to open the envelope in her hand! But she needed to share with her family, if it turned out to be good news. And if it wasn't good news, she would need her family even more. She suddenly wanted her family more than ever.

Turning her gaze back to the envelope in her hand, Jackie found it was gone, and a cell phone was in its place. A message was coming through, but try as she might, she couldn't read the words; they seemed to float off the screen before she could focus on them. Her eyelids drooped. It was useless. She somehow knew this message was urgent, but could not make it out. Frantic, she began to type out a text. She would text each member of her family until someone came to help her, to read the messages, to open the envelope, to tell her what to do next. Someone would come to help her. Jackie typed and typed.

Larry sat by Jackie's bedside in their comfortable bedroom. He counted the clear drops coming from the IV bag, to make sure they were spaced at the right number of drops per minute. Thank goodness their insurance afforded them a part-time nurse. She came twice each day to administer the drugs that kept Jackie nourished and sleeping, so she could recover at home. Jackie had become so weak that some really bad things had started to attack her body, things that a healthy body would have just brushed off. A healthy person has a T-cell count of around one thousand or higher. The doctor said Jackie's T-cells had dropped to 8! They had to rebuild that number before they could rebuild her body. They were monitoring her T-cells carefully. Larry was grateful that she was sedated. It had become clear this was the only way to keep her from obsessing and working and worrying herself to death. But he missed her. Larry propped his chin on his hand and his eyes grew heavy. The last thing he saw before he fell asleep was quite odd: The fingers on Jackie's left hand, the one that wasn't hooked up to the tubes, were fluttering in the air, as if she was frantically typing something.

The Christmas tree was drooping, a spray of dead needles on the floor beneath it. The lights were still strung, but no longer blinking. Stephanie stood, phone pressed to her ear, and stared at the skeletal remains. It occurred to her that a tree, taken from its natural habitat, would die. Jason, too, would not survive prison. He would wither until all the lights had gone dark.

OK, now the phone was ringing. Stephanie knew it was not the best idea to burden Jackie with this news, but she would have to know sooner or later. And since the doctors had released her from their care, Jackie seemed stronger than ever. Please pick up. "Ms. Jackie, please pick up — Jackie? Are you there?"

A metallic click was followed by Jackie's familiar, "Hey there!"

Stephanie became instantly animated and burst into speech. "Jim just called me from the arraignment."

Oddly, Jackie was speaking over Stephanie, who then heard Jackie invite her to, "Leave a message after the beep!"

Jackie always kept her cell phone nearby, especially now. She must be scrambling to find the phone in the bottom of her pocketbook, or maybe she was just stepping out of the shower. Stephanie would call back later. But then she heard the beep and began to spill her feelings to Jackie's voicemail. "Jackie, Jim just called me from the arraignment. Are you there? Did they let you go to the arraignment? Jackie, pick up. The DA, this Evelyn Pitt, has added five more charges! It's felony murder and felony possession and aggravated assault and — and the judge asked her to please reduce the charges but she insisted — are you there? Ms. Jackie? Please be there. Please pick up. Somebody talk to me. Somebody — "

Abruptly she ceased to speak, but continued to hold the phone firmly to her ear. She wasn't sure if she was still being recorded or not. Stephanie looked up to see JJ standing in the shadows of the hallway.

This was a very unusual night, in the deep winter of early 2009. Unusual for Jim and Jennifer, as the house was quiet. All three girls were at an overnight slumber party. Jennifer was using this time to organize the girls' room. At one point, there had been a toy box for toys and closets for clothes. A place for everything. Now the entire room was filled with little dresses, stuffed animals, posters, toys, books, and memorabilia. Jennifer had spent a great deal of time designing the room and now it was only a jumble of youthful femininity. Cute, but jumbled.

Perhaps it was only the solitude or looking over the finger paintings, clippings, and clutter that her daughters had accrued, but Jennifer suddenly felt a nostalgic tug. Seemed like only yesterday, she could not have imagined the girls staying away from home all night. And heavens, things like dating had always been situated in some nebulous future, surely light years away. Seeing Hannah so mature and responsible had recently brought home the fact that Anna Grace would soon be maturing as well and then little Pay-Pay — Jennifer did not realize she was crying. She had no idea why Jim was suddenly in the room with a pained look on his face. She watched his reflection in the mirror and attempted to ask what was the matter, but all that came out was an empty sob. Jennifer pitched forward on the little padded chair, face down onto the dresser top as her shoulders began to heave. Jim drew near, and rested his hand on her neck, but he didn't say a word until the tears began to subside. When she was better, he helped dry her eyes with a doll dress. Then he pulled up a little chair and sat next to her. When she was ready, she began to speak. "You know how a river digs down into the earth and washes away the ground slowly by specks of dirt and grains of sand for centuries and centuries? That's how life is. You go through every day, just rolling on like a river, and you don't realize what has changed and worn away until you look back. Because it happened so slowly. You don't even notice. Our girls are getting so big. But they're not big enough to deal with what is happening to our family. I am not big enough to deal with it. And I think we're about to get a shock. We're used to slow erosion and we're okay with that. But I'm afraid we're about to have a flood, or a — what do you call those things that —?"

"Avalanche?" Jim guessed.

"No, it's like water and it's...."

"Tsunami?

"That's it!" Jennifer practically shouted. "We've been used to a slow, rolling river and we're about to get a tsunami! What is that going to do to Stephanie and JJ?! And to us?! I was thinking about the girls getting older and then I thought what if Jason goes to jail for thirty years and I suddenly saw JJ, clear as a bell. He was all grown up with children of his own and didn't know the old man who finally got out of jail and told JJ to call him daddy."

Jennifer began to weep again, but this time slow, aching sobs. She finally choked out, "We have to do something...something!"

"Honey. What can we do?"

"I don't know, but something!"

"Okay. We can pray. We can let them know we are here for them. Can you think of anything else?"

76

"No. You're right. It's just that lately I wish....."

"Go on, Jennifer. Say it."

"I love that you're doing God's work. But at times like this, I wish you were CEO instead of middle management."

Jennifer looked up to see Jim's face stunned; completely immobile. Why had she said that? What a horrible thing to say! And then Jim took a deep breath and out came one of the loudest laughs she had ever heard. A real gut buster. He gasped and tried to catch his breath, but the laughter had overtaken him. It took a moment, but Jennifer finally allowed herself a smile, then a giggle. And then they fell into each other's arms and laughed until they cried and then laughed some more. Thumper, ill at ease over this strange behavior by his parents, watched them for a moment, tail tucked. Then he cut loose with a low baneful, "Woooooooooooooooo?"

And they were off again.

Chapter Nine

Choices

This being a weekday, there were no services at Jim's church. It was a small church, which was just the way Jim wanted it. He and Jennifer were able to get to know all the people who gathered there. It was a place of family, even for those who did not have a family. Jim didn't care for the phrase, "preach at," but preferred, "worship with." And so they did, each and every Sunday and Wednesday night. But being a weekday, the church was empty. Almost. One car was in the parking lot. Inside, Jason and Stephanie knelt in front of the altar that bore the words, *This do in remembrance of me.* * From any distance, it would have been difficult to tell if the kneeling couple were talking or thinking or praying. They were very still for a long time. The church was still.

Then, at exactly the same instant, they both raised their heads and looked at one another. They were smiling and nodding and Steph was

---

* **KJV Luke 22:19**

wiping away tears. Jason rose and helped his wife to her feet. Holding hands like sweethearts, they walked down the aisle towards the front doors. Stopping at the last pew, they turned their attention to JJ, sitting small and all alone. Then they looked at one another again and smiled. Jason began to speak to his son, "JJ. We've reached a decision about the trial. We want to explain something. You know that with one choice I go to jail for three years. With the other choice I risk going to jail for thirty years, but with this second choice I might not go to jail at all. We just don't know. Now there's something else about this second choice; something that has become very important to us. By taking that choice, we would be allowed to speak. We would be able to tell the whole world what really happened. But we'd also be risking being separated until... until you are as old as I am now."

Stephanie took up the thread, "It's really important that the world knows your daddy would never intentionally hurt anyone. It means a lot to us that the world knows you have a good father. And we hope —"

Jason finished her sentence, "We hope that a jury — the people who decide what happens to me — would also see that I didn't mean to hurt anyone. It would be good to tell everyone the truth. But by doing that, we would be taking a terrible risk. A terrible risk."

"It's taken us a long time, JJ," Stephanie continued to try to explain. "We have prayed and discussed and searched. And we know now what we have to do to bring us peace."

"You're going to trial," JJ said simply.

Jason and Stephanie exchanged an almost comical look of amazement.

"Yes, we are," Jason stammered, "but how did you know?"

"Sometimes you just gotta stand and fight."

As the parents of three small girls, Jim and Jennifer had perfected Parent Speak. (Just in case you don't know the meaning of the phrase, here it is: Parent Speak allows adults to discuss sensitive issues without revealing too much to their offspring. Parent Speak consists of half-sentences, sentences with an offending word left out, half-swallowed phrases, meaningful and exaggerated facial expressions, and sentences that fade into nothing or are muffled behind hands or napkins. Real pros can hide iffy words behind a cough.) Tonight, around the dinner table, Jim and Jennifer had some heavy issues to discuss and were in full PS mode as the girls enjoyed their dinner.

"I knew," Jennifer passed her napkin over her mouth and spoke from behind it, "...umm hmm would take it hard..."

"What else," Jim cleared his throat, "could...do?"

"But so long....drawn out."

"Other way...worse..."

"Knew she'd....push...too hard."

"Trying to do it all...self."

"Can't blame...I mean...own son."

"She never did trust," Jim spoke into his water glass, "lawyers."

"Up *all night*....," Jennifer mouthed the word, "internet."

"Piles of law books...stacks..."

"Saw this coming...told you..."

"I don't think....had anything to do with...."

"'Course it did! Hasn't...had a good night's sleep..."

"Coulda happened to anybody."

Between bites of mashed potatoes, Patience demanded, "What coulda happened?"

Jennifer raised her eyebrows disapprovingly. "Don't speak with your mouth full. Nothing baby."

Patience persisted, "Will it happen to me?!"

"No, baby."

Jim tried to assure Patience with, "This is a...."

Jennifer began, "This is just a...."

Hannah put down her fork and wiped her mouth before speaking. "Gommi was afraid the lawyers don't know how to help Uncle Bird so she tried to study all the law books to find out how to keep him from going to jail but she worried too much and couldn't sleep and that made her tired and sick and she ran her car off the road and now she's in the hospital where they'll make her stay in bed and rest and feed her dinner through a straw."

Hannah addressed her parents' dumbfounded stares with, "Seriously, Mom, we're not children."

Anna Grace added, "Not children."

Looking at her meatloaf, Patience asked for a straw.

It was true that the doctors saved Jackie's life. But the impending trial and the seemingly constant bad news (including the new charges for Jason) wore Jackie back down. Jason and Stephanie's decision to risk a jury trial had sent Jackie right back to her law books. She kept looking for the right book to give her the perfect answer. The car accident left her in the hospital where she was forced to recover; to think and to search and to pray. After her release, she was more fragile, physically, but much stronger spiritually and emotionally. She also seemed to realize that if she didn't take better care of herself, she would be of no use to anyone. For the first time, she understood that her own weakness might have been detrimental to the entire situation and to everyone involved.

Jackie has since declared that she died and was reborn. For so long she had tried to take care of everything. But one day as she sat in church, completely alone, something miraculous happened. She gave up. She simply told her Heavenly Father that she could do no more. These were not simply words; she truly gave up. She gave everything over to Him. And in that moment of brokenness and spiritual death, she was reborn. By giving everything up, she gained all. Her stubbornness and willfulness had given way to complete humility, and her tiny seed of faith was spectacularly grown into a tree of faith that drank of the waters of eternity. Oh, the mountain was still before her, but now there were moments of hope.

Now her reactions and plans were quite sane and well-thought out. She spent time planning for the trial, praying alone in Jim's church, and reading a book she had found in a little pharmacy on her first day of freedom. *Psalm 91 - God's Shield Of Protection* seemed to give her focus, and she spent a great deal of time with the book and in Psalms. Jackie stated that she had moved into the book of Psalms, and was living there. And one night, after clearing out all the law books and files and notes from the living room, she sat reading her Bible. What had been true all along became exquisitely clear to her: With all the searching and studying she had been doing over all these months, she had been looking in the wrong book.

It was a stark, icy day in early 2009 when Jackie approached Larry with an idea. She wanted to call Michael Kam and bluntly ask him what else he would do if he were in this situation. In fact, *is* there anything to do? He only had one suggestion: a mock trial. This would be constructed like a real trial, except the jurors and members of the court would be hired. Kam and another lawyer would try Jason's case; Kam using exactly the arguments he intended to use in court. The "jurors" would deliberate and a verdict would be reached. And it would cost $100,000.00 to produce. One hundred thousand. When Jackie heard Kam pronounce the cost over the speaker phone, she turned to look at Larry, but he was nowhere to be found. Larry had quietly gone to get his check book. There was no hesitation; if it would help, Larry would see that it was done.

From the moment Larry wrote that check, until the day that the mock trial began, Jackie wondered if she had made a mistake. After all, this was no guarantee of anything. If they exonerated Jason and sent him home in the mock trial, would that set them all up for an even greater fall if, at the real trial, Jason was.... She wouldn't let herself think of it. And yet, if the mock jurors convicted Jason — what then? Would Jason and Stephanie back out of the real trial? Could they still take the plea bargain? At times, Jackie felt as if her brain had simply stalled; it just wouldn't accept another thought or idea and instead sat idling and humming and useless. Those were the times that she found her way to her prayer closet. With only the glow of the nightlights to guide her, and being careful not to step on her dogs, she would walk or crawl to the solitude of her closet. There, by the light of a candle, she would pray to God to give her strength to let go. "How ridiculous," she thought out loud on one particular night. "That doesn't make any sense. The *strength* to *let go*? Letting go means giving up or giving over and how could you possibly need strength to quit being strong? And if you need strength to quit being strong....."

Jackie had no idea how long she had been pondering this conundrum, but when Larry came to guide her back to bed, the sky was getting light.

The mock trial was grueling for everyone. Detailed and complex, it was easy to forget this wasn't the real thing. If the mock trial tore them to shreds, as it was doing, how would they survive the real thing? When the mock trial "jury" was finally sent to deliberate, the family was called into a hidden room. There, through the use of computers and hidden cameras and microphones, the family was able to see and hear the entire painful procedure. The mock jurors seemed intelligent and impartial. Jackie mentioned that she was amazed how they were able to remember the trial in such detail. They discussed and argued and worked endlessly.

Michael Kam had reminded his clients that all twelve jurors must find Jason innocent of all charges if he was to be acquitted and come home to them. Over all, the mock jurors seem to be sympathetic to Jason's situation, but as the family was finding out, jurors are also bound by the law. And torn between opinion and the law, jurors are sometimes forced to reach a verdict that they don't entirely agree with. It was insanity! As the test trial drew on, the overwhelming weight of their situation wore on the family. In the end, it was worse than Kam had predicted: Every single juror found Jason guilty of something.

As they walked to the car, Jackie felt hostile toward everyone and everything. Larry offered his hand but she brushed him away. She was trying to hold all the bad feelings at bay, but they were bullying her; demanding attention. Slamming the passenger door, she turned and stared out the window. Why weren't they headed home? Why didn't he start the engine and drive away from this place? Jackie jerked her head around to glare at Larry. He was simply sitting and waiting on her. He was holding his checkbook as he spoke to her, "Do you want them to do another one?"

Sometimes there is no explanation for love. No words. It just is; indomitable and eternal. In that moment, seeing Larry's calm and clear offer to pay anything to help his wife and this man who wasn't even his son, Jackie felt the power of love calm her body and steady her mind.

She took the check book from her husband and put it firmly away. Then they held hands as they drove home.

On a blustery Wednesday, two little boys in identical school uniforms walked toward home. Wyatt liked spending time with JJ and hoped he was JJ's best friend. Although JJ had forgotten the comment Wyatt made about his dad in class, (much bigger thoughts crowded JJ's mind) Wyatt wanted to make sure that his friend understood it was a mistake. Because Wyatt lived on the other side of the Veitch home, he would often stop at JJ's to "rest." Of course this was just an excuse for the two of them to play video games until Stephanie called them to supper. A burst of wind threatened to lift Wyatt's cap off his head, but he managed to grab it and pull it down further on his head. Fascinated by the idea of someone he knew being a part of a trial, he suddenly had another question for JJ. "Will you get to watch the trial?"

"No, Deddy says no little kids."

"That don't seem fair. He's your daddy."

"But I get to go when they pick the jury!"

"What's picking the jury?"

"I don't know. But I get to go."

And without warning, Travis Vertue and one of his goons stood in their path. "Hey, Jailbird. Hear your daddy's goin' up for a long time," Travis taunted loudly. "Up the river!"

Under his breath, JJ instructed Wyatt to, "Just keep walking."

"Maybe they make your mama go to jail, too. What you gonna do then, Jailbird?"

JJ was cornered, trying to decide what to do, when Wyatt spoke up steady and clear. "His daddy is not going to jail, he's going to *trial.*"

"What you know about it, Beaner, you ain't even American."

Wyatt walked the remaining two feet and spoke right into Travis' face, "I'm just as American as you are."

Without warning, Travis punched the much smaller boy squarely in the face, sending Wyatt reeling. JJ moved in protectively, kneeling beside his friend. Travis and his thug moved in for the kill. But instead of covering his head and waiting for the blows, JJ pulled himself up and stood as tall as he was able. "Travis Vertue, you're a bully."

"What?!"

"You. Are. A. Bully."

"So?" Travis was clearly angered and flustered. He was used to speaking with his fists and with taunts and threats. Conversation was not his strong suit.

JJ answered, "So, a bully is nothing but a coward. You're a coward and a bully."

"What? Say *what?!*"

"And there's only two things to do about a bully. Only two ways to find peace. And I already tried one."

"So what'd'ya think you're gonna do now?"

"I think I'm gonna punch your lights out."

Two little boys in identical school uniforms walked home from school. Behind them, Travis was sprawled, bloodied and stunned, on the sidewalk. His goon was running rapidly in the other direction. As they walked away, the boys could hear Travis crying.

Trying to keep up with JJ's stride, Wyatt asked, "Did punching his lights out give you peace, JJ?" They walked on in silence as JJ considered this for a moment. Then a broad grin broke out on his face. The boys threw their arms around each other's shoulders and walked home, strong and smiling.

Chapter Ten

It Begins

Courtroom B of the Crockett County Courthouse was a small, plain room. Too small, in fact, for the crowd trying to wedge themselves into the narrow aisles. The Carpenter and Veitch families were assembled for the selection of jurors. The man on the bench sat behind a black and gold plaque which informed everyone that this was JUDGE T. BURTON. A court reporter sat beside the judge. At a small table below the judge, and to his right, were Jason, Ellis Burdette, and Defense Attorney Michael Kam. Larry looked at the pleasant, dignified man with a trim, silver beard and recalled that he had a very different image in mind when he had first heard the name, Michael Kam. Kam was nothing like Larry's first mental image of the inscrutable, wise, Asian man with all the answers.

At the table below Judge Burton and to his left sat Prosecuting Attorney Evelyn Pitt. Seated next to Ms. Pitt, Jackie and Stephanie recognized Gus Crutcher. Jason's parents were seated directly behind

Jason and it distressed Jackie that she could not see his face. Jim and Stephanie sat with the Carpenters, as did JJ, dressed in a suit that was smaller, but otherwise identical to his dad's.

To the family's right and behind Pitt and Crutcher were potential jurors. Filling up the remainder of the seats were onlookers, many of them representatives of the Hispanic community. Members of the press stood against the walls on three sides of the room, and the swinging double doors in back were open so those packed into the hallway could see and hear.

Judge Burton finished perusing a stack of papers before him and looked up over half-glasses. He was soft-spoken, easy; even grandfatherly in manner. Jason wondered if this man could even imagine what it would be like to be in a defendant's place.

Judge Burton began to speak. "Ladies and Gentlemen, welcome. This is a Crockett County murder case that you may be selected to hear. Before you're asked any questions by the court or by the counsel, I must give you what's called the voir dire oath. And for that oath I ask you to please stand and raise your right hand."

A surprising number of people rose, raising their hands. Those still seated craned their necks to get a look at the potential jurors.

Judge Burton began, "You shall give true answers to all questions as may be asked by the court or its authority including all questions asked by the parties or their attorney concerning your qualifications as jurors in the case of the State of Georgia versus Richard Jason Veitch, so help you God."

And there it was. After all these months, it was happening. This was real and Jason and every member of his family were struck by the formidable power of the words being spoken. "The State of Georgia versus...." So the entire state was against Jason. Yes, that's how it had felt; the judge only confirmed it.

Six hours later, the stress of jury selection showed clearly on the family. JJ, however, like many of the onlookers, just seemed tired and bored. A potential juror, a Mrs. Moncada, was standing. When she spoke, it was with a very heavy dialect. Even after all these hours, Jason and his family took in everything with keen eyes and ears. Some of the people in this room, some of these people answering questions today, would decide Jason's fate. They would have control over his life, and the lives of anyone who cared for him. Ellis, too, watched rigid and tense. Only Michael Kam seemed relaxed.

Prosecuting Attorney Evelyn Pitt was such a pretty, slim young woman. Her pastel suit and gently upswept hair were matched perfectly by her soothing voice and Georgia peach complexion. She was addressing Mrs. Moncada. "...and how long have you lived in this country, Mrs. Moncada?"

"About seven years."

"And how long have you lived in Crockett County?"

"In this country?"

"No, Mrs. Moncada, in this *county*; in Crockett Coun —"

"Oh, *oh*, I live for two, no, yes, two years here in county."

"Are you familiar with the Jason Veitch case?"

"No. Not familiar."

JJ had been drowsy earlier and he wasn't sure if he had nodded off against his mother's shoulder or not. Now he was fully awake, and worse: he was bored. He had seen everything there was to see in this room and little itchy needles kept telling him to move his legs. He checked to see if there was anything else to count. There were squares in the ceiling with little holes in them and after every fourth square was a square light. After every square third light was a square air vent. There was nothing to count on the carpet. And the doors, except for their red signs, were plain. And people were talking about things he didn't understand and nobody laughed or smiled. He wondered how long it took a jury to pick and what they were picking. Bored.

His truck! His truck was in his mama's purse! He began to dig into the mysterious depths when Stephanie gave him the eye. So he dug very, very quietly, and there it was - that cool, solid metal! He carefully removed his treasure and began to examine it. But that didn't take long. Nothing new here.

JJ stood quietly and balanced his truck on the back of the seats in front of him. The seats were long benches, like at church, so he was able to drive his truck, without disturbing anyone, the length of the bench and to the aisle. Usually he made noises for his cars, trucks, and dinosaurs, but today he only made the noises in his head. After driving the truck to the aisle, he was able to see the other half of the courtroom much better. And there, just on the other side, was an old friend! He could only see him in profile, but there was no mistaking him. This was the man who had delivered his truck from the heights of the hardware store shelves. JJ stared until he caught Jose Lerma's attention and sent him a wave and a broad smile. Jose didn't seem to see him. JJ waited for another opportunity and this time, he lifted his truck for his friend to see. Lerma looked at the truck, up to JJ, back to the truck and then turned his attention back to the front of the courtroom. Why didn't this man recognize him? What was so important to him that he kept staring at the people who were talking and talking in the front? JJ ducked and, mostly unobserved, crossed the aisle.

He entered the row behind Lerma, and quietly drove his truck along the top of Lerma's bench until it was directly behind him. Before he could whisper or tap the man on his shoulder, an older woman seated next to Lerma caught JJ's attention. The woman's outfit was clean but worn and she had been crying. In her hand she held a framed photograph of a smiling young man in graduation cap and gown. With a crumpled handkerchief, she was gently wiping the glass. JJ recognized the photo as one of the men who had been in the hardware store with his new friend!

Michael Kam had begun to interview Mrs. Moncada in a relaxed, folksy manner. "Mrs. Moncada, are any members of Jason Veitch's family known to you?"

"Pardon?"

"Do you know this man seated here at this table; do you know Jason Veitch?"

"Oh, no, no; I don't know him."

"Was Mr. Juan Carlos Reymundo known to you?"

At the mention of the name Juan Carlos Reymundo, the woman with the framed photograph made a funny little sound in her throat and pressed the handkerchief to her mouth. JJ watched her for a moment.

Mrs. Moncada answered, "No, I no know him."

Kam continued slowly but steadily, "Do you know any members of Mr. Reymundo's family?"

"No."

"Mrs. Moncada, are you aware that Juan Carlos Reymundo was killed with a shotgun blast to his back on the night of February 29, 2008?"

This time at the mention of Juan Carlos Reymundo, the woman began to weep anew and her tears fell on the picture of the man JJ had seen in the hardware store.

"Yes."

"And are you aware that Jason Veitch has been accused of killing Mr. Reymundo?"

"Yes."

"And yet earlier you said that you were not familiar with this case..."

The last words JJ heard clearly were his daddy's name, and "killing Mr. Reymundo."

JJ looked at the man sitting next to Lerma. It was the third man who had been in the hardware store. So two of the men were here. And the picture of the third man was here. And a woman was crying over a picture of the third man, but he wasn't here. The child's mind finally put all the pieces together. His face burned. He wanted to go home. He wanted to still be sitting by his mama. JJ turned to see Lerma staring at him, staring right into his eyes. For one brief eternity the man and boy looked at one another. Then, leaving his truck behind, JJ turned and walked back to his seat.

It was a Moose day. JJ sat on his front porch waiting for the big man to arrive, Bible in hand, for his regular talk with JJ's dad. As a rule now, Moose always sat down on the porch beside JJ before going inside, and Jason never interrupted their talks or urged them to hurry. JJ usually had to take the lead and begin their chats, so sometimes they just sat in silence for a while. JJ felt good sitting next to the big man. He somehow felt that, if someone tried to take his daddy away, Moose would stand up and rip open his shirt like his favorite superhero and save them all.

The little boy had never seen the big man do anything out of anger, but he was pretty certain Moose could swell up and turn green if provoked.

This day was cold but sunny, and Moose did not sit on his usual side of the porch, but moved to the opposite side, so as not to block the sun's warmth from his little friend. It had been over a year since that terrible night in the woods. So much had changed. JJ had bunches of questions for his parents, but he also saw how sad and busy they were, so he was glad he had Moose, too.

"Mr. Moose, why do you always call me Mr. JJ?"

"Why do you always call me Mr. Moose?"

"My mama and deddy always told me to call grownups Mr. and Miz. Or Miss."

"Do you think I'm grown up?"

"Yessir. Don't you?"

"I never thought about it. I don't feel grownup. I feel like everybody is smarter than me or better'n me. Never thought of myself as a grownup."

"But don't you have a little boy of your own?"

"I do."

"Well you have to be a grownup to have your own kids, right?"

"Not according to his mama."

"What's his mama say?"

"She says, 'Moose, you ain't never grown up and you ain't never gonna grow up and you're bad for the boy. And I won't have you messing up his life like you messed up yours.'"

JJ sat quietly, turning this over in his mind. It surprised him when Moose spoke up with this additional observation: "I reckon you can be big without being a grownup. I reckon."

"Does your boy's mama know that you're good now?"

"*Trying* to be good."

"Does his mama know that you're *trying* to be good?"

"I don't reckon she knows. I ain't seen her in a good while."

"Maybe you should let her know."

"Don't see no use in that. I done what I done. Nothing good could come of it."

JJ chose his words very carefully. "Mr. Moose, are you glad you met my deddy?"

"I sure am. Every day. Real glad."

"But if he didn't get put in jail, you never would have met him, right?"

"Right."

"So something real good came of it. Something bad had to happen so that something good could happen."

Moose turned and looked down at JJ, so small and yet so intense and wise. The man's voice sounded funny when he said, "Maybe you're right."

"And if you go and show your boy's mama that you are trying to be good, and got to see your boy again, that would be another good thing that came from my deddy having trouble."

"But I ain't sure where she is."

"Ain't you even gonna try?"

"Don't say ain't."

"Aresn't you even gonna try?"

Moose seemed to be looking at something far away, way across the street and past the Rawls' house.

JJ spoke again. "I been talking to Jesus. And I think my deddy's going to get to come home for good. I don't know when, but someday probably. And when he does, I want him to hear about all the good things that happened because of his bad times. He is real sad and so is my mama, but I think they'd be happy if they could see all the good things coming from the suffering."

"Good things?"

"Yeah, like us getting to know you and me learning all about bullies and how to stand up to them and getting to be friends with Wyatt and maybe you getting your little boy back. And I bet there will be more. Bad stuff turns into good stuff. Like after the flood, God gave us a rainbow. And he's still giving us rainbows."

Moose got up and walked into the house without a word. But JJ knew he wasn't mad. He knew it.

The date was set. Michael Kam notified Jason that the trial was set to begin on Monday the 13th of April 2009, and Stephanie phoned the other family members immediately. Jason and Stephanie had discussed this eventuality and how to handle it. They had made the decision that brought them peace, and whenever the date for the trial was set, it would give them hope; something solid to work toward. Something real. But it didn't feel that way now that the date was set; now that it was real. Jason felt as if the earth had suddenly been pulled out from beneath him. Stephanie tried to stay busy. JJ sensed the change instantaneously. People began to come to their house, and it wasn't just people he knew like Moose and Mr. Ellis. No, it was people in suits and people who spoke in hushed tones and used big words. One stranger reminded JJ of the man with big eyebrows at the Shepherd's Funeral Home; both were tall and thin and their voices were filled with shadows. Each day, JJ reminded himself of what he could do to help: 1) He could try to not be a pain to his parents, 2) He could talk to Jesus about his daddy, 3) He could show his daddy how much he loved him, and 4) JJ could look real hard at his daddy; hard as he could. This way, in case he didn't get to really look at him some day, he would have lots of memories.

Jim and Jennifer found a surprisingly large number of things they were able to help with. In addition to picking up JJ for extra time with the girls, they were able to run errands and do menial jobs that would allow Steph and Jason to tend to the multitude of details that had suddenly become urgent. Jason informed his brother that he had spent some time with Steph, educating her about finances, contracts, and other tasks that she might be faced with. Jason also gave his big brother a list of things to check on for a while, just till Stephanie and JJ got used to a new routine. It was brutal to think of the worst-case scenario, but it had to be done.

Jim had grown quite proficient at deflecting comments that could lead back to Jason's situation or become inflammatory. Jim and Jen also continued to keep the girls updated and educated, in case they were goaded for a comment. The parents filtered the information, of course, being careful to present issues in such a way that the girls could easily digest it. Hannah was quite mature in her response to the entire situation; her parents knew that she grieved for her aunt and uncle and cousin, but outwardly she kept a good, sensible attitude about it. They were all learning to keep certain things private, avoid specific subjects, and to deflect when necessary. This new talent that the family was compelled to learn led to a rather comic event one winter evening. And if the comment had come from Hannah, it would not have surprised her parents. But it didn't come from Hannah or even Anna Grace, it came from little Pay-Pay.

During the church Winter-Fest, Jim was filling plastic cups with punch and behind him was a big curtain with letters cut from colorful construction paper. After a moment, he recognized his daughter's voice coming from the other side of the curtain. It seemed Patience had been confronted by some of the older "mean girls" that always seem to run in packs. They say there's safety in numbers, and it could also be said that it takes a bunch to bully. Cowards rarely act alone, and bullies are cowards. In sneering tones (Jim recognized the little girl's voice, but never did reveal her identity to Jennifer) the child told Patience that her mom had told her, that criminal *tendatsies* ran in families, which means that Patience's mom or dad would probably do something awful someday just like Jason. Pay-Pay's tremulous voice asked the leader of the pack if that was really true. "Yes," the girl decreed, "Your uncle killed somebody, so that means that JJ will too, and you probably will too. Because you have *tendatsies.*"

Patience' voice was broken as she asked, "Does that mean that we are going to grow up to be just like our parents?"

"It certainly does, Patience Veitch!" the older girl proclaimed.

No longer sounding tearful, Patience quipped, "Oh, so that means you're going to be fat and bald, huh?"

Now Jim didn't usually champion cruelty, but the last year had taught him some things. He had learned that sometimes you had to fight fire with fire; sometimes you had to stand your ground. And Patience had only responded in kind, using the same tools as the older girl. Besides, the little brat's crimson face as she stormed out assured Jim that she would think twice before bullying again. And that's a good thing.

Jackie had a date. She had a deadline. She had something to do. Jackie was, to her fingertips, an organizer; she needed a cause. And now she had a very big one.

The first thing she did was start organizing closets for the trial. She began on the left side of her closet, with a dress on a hanger, shoes below, stockings, belt — anything she would need for court — in one spot. She didn't want anything as mundane as searching for a purse to slow her down. If the trial ran too long, she'd simply start back at the left side of the closet and work her way down again.

Jackie had been sternly warned not to bring her Bible to court, because it might offend non-believers. So for her first day in court, she chose a brazen red dress, knowing her Bible would be clearly seen against that color. She was not so concerned about the non-believers as she was the believers, and she would make a prominent entrance with her Bible as the shield of protection for her family.

Next, she went to Larry's closet. Each suit had a matching shirt and tie and shoes. She stuffed socks into the shoes and cuff links into the jacket pockets.

Jackie tore Psalm 91 out of her Bible and gave it to Stephanie, with instructions to place it into Jason's jacket each day of the trial. She made sure that Larry had her car and the SUV checked from top to bottom. Nothing would stop her from being in the courtroom, on time, and prepared. If this was war, she would be a warrior. During the past months, she had seen Satan frolic and dance upon God's children and she had learned some things. Jackie had always believed that God could do all things, but she had learned that He really likes it when we help.

This morning was reminiscent of earlier mornings in the Veitch sisters' bedroom. But this morning, all the girls were quiet and subdued. Jennifer stood mid-room, as if trying to remember something. Hannah helped dress Patience, as Anna Grace studied her reflection in the dresser mirror and tried different hairstyles. Jennifer jumped slightly at the sound of Patience's sudden question, "Can I go to court, too?"

Distracted, "No, Sweetie, it's just for grownups."

"What about school?"

"Since Mommy won't be here to teach you today, you get a day off from school."

"Does JJ get a day off?"

"No, Baby, JJ isn't home-schooled; he goes to private school."

Anna Grace turned away from the mirror, hand still holding her hair atop her head. "Is Gommi going to stay with us today, Mom?"

"Mr. Moose is going to stay with you today, while Mommy is at the courthouse. Then tomorrow I'll stay with you, then maybe the next day Poppi will stay here. We all want to be with your Uncle Jason during the trial, so we'll take turns staying with you."

Patience whined, "I want to go be with Uncle Bird."

Hannah finished the buttons on Pay-Pay's outfit as she spoke, "You can't go to court. Court is like Disneyland: You have to be 'this tall' to go to court."

"Now, girls," Jennifer began, "Do you think you can play nice while Mr. Moose is staying with you?"

Hannah appeared to be deep in thought. Anna Grace shot her mom a look in the mirror. Patience just smiled.

Just hours later, the girls were seated in teeny tiny chairs around a teeny tiny table. Each appeared to be attired for a ritzy social affair, with wardrobe designed primarily by Anna Grace, who was wearing her mom's best Sunday hat, heels, and pearls. Moose, also seated in a tiny chair, was wearing a tiara and feather boa. Thumper circled the tea party waiting for imaginary crumbs from imaginary tea cakes to drop on the floor. Patience eyed Moose critically over her tiny teacup before speaking. "Why don't you got any hair?"

"I got hair," Moose replied casually.

"But your head is shiny."

"I cut it off."

"Can I cut my hair off?"

Hannah spoke up, "Mr. Moose, did you see our uncle when you were at the courthouse, and no, Patience, you cannot cut off your hair."

"Yes, I did."

Anna Grace put down her cup and asked, "Does he miss us?"

"I reckon."

Hannah thought for a moment before asking, "Is he scared?"

"I dunno."

"Didn't you ask him?" ventured Anna Grace.

"They won't let him talk to us. Until the trial is over, they won't let him talk to anybody but Miz Stephanie."

And then, all were silent. Nobody sipped their tea. Silence. Moose munched on a make-believe cookie and spoke up, "You know what your Uncle Jason did today?"

All eyes on Moose. "Some bad people said things that weren't true. And I got mad. But your Uncle Jason didn't. He just kept on telling the truth. And the more they tried to make him mad, the more he just spoke easy and told the truth. And you know who ended up mad? Those bad people."

The party seemed to be back on, and Hannah refreshed the tea for each guest. Moose delicately sipped his tea as he added, "One of those bad people got so mad, she blew snot out of her nose."

The girls shrieked with laughter, but Moose, retaining his composure, simply adjusted his tiara.

Chapter Eleven

Praying for Rainbows

⌒〜⌒

L ate winter in Georgia can be tricky. Spring might just creep in and surprise you. Then again, you could get comfortable with the warmer weather, and — bam! — Blackberry Winter comes in with a frigid blast. This was the first year that JJ was acutely aware of the passage of time. He could remember how drastically his world had changed at the end of last February, how life battered him in March, and exactly what was happening within his family in the middle of April, 2008. But this was April 2009. He'd learned a lot in one year. JJ found that some folks won't like you, no matter what you do, and other folks will always like you, no matter what you do. And you can turn some people around, but not all. And if you can't turn them around, you turn away. But if they won't let you turn away, you stand up to them. While last spring had been filled with fear and change and sadness, life seemed all clear now to this seven-year-old. He knew how to handle bullies, could ride a bike, had learned what the words "racist" and "privileged" and "prejudiced" meant, and he was finally doing well in math. Yep, he guessed he just about had life all figured out.

His daddy was just standing up to bullies, as he had done. But the bullies that went after his daddy were crafty and sly and there was a big bunch of them. Being grownups, they had learned much more about how to hurt people. So this fight was taking a long time. When spring was breaking last year, he didn't know what a trial was; now he knew all too well about trials and jury selection and courtrooms. He was well aware that, in just a few days, his daddy would go to trial. And in many ways, he and his family would go to trial as well. JJ had been told that he couldn't go to the courtroom and watch; that he must continue his studies. If only the trial had happened during summer vacation! He believed that he could help Jason by being in the courtroom, but he innately understood that everyone in his family had a job to do. His job was to go to school and study hard and be a good boy. And talk to Jesus about keeping His wings of protection over his family. That's what his Gommi called it: God's wings of protection. And sometimes she talked about being safe because He tells us, *He shall give his angels charge over thee.* * Jackie found those words in JJ's favorite Bible book, the book of Psalms. So he knew it was true.

April 13, the first day of Jason's trial, would be Monday. On this Saturday, April 11, JJ and Hannah and Anna Grace and Patience were spending the day with their Gommi and Poppi. After lunch, the children left their grandparents in the house and went out to play in the rolling hills behind the house. The house itself was situated high on a hill, so the rise above and behind the house afforded quite a view. This day was warm and breezy and the air was filled with the scent of honeysuckle and the drowsy drone of bees. When little children become grownups, this is the type day they like to remember when they look back on their childhood. Days like this one felt endless. After some romping and running and burning off energy, the four youngsters fell into the soft grass. Lying on their backs, the brilliant sky presented them

---

*   **KJV Psalm 91:11**

with an ever-changing panorama of cloud figures and cloud animals and fluffy white vistas.

Pay-Pay asked no one in particular, "Where do clouds go when they go away?"

JJ offered, "Maybe they go to heaven. Yeah, that's it. They go to heaven and God recycles them and sends them back. Like maybe one of these white clouds will come back as a storm cloud."

Hannah was more realistic. "They get recycled all right. They turn into dew or mist or rain. And then they evaporate and go up in the sky and become clouds again."

Patience considered this and responded, "I like what JJ said better."

And of course, Anna Grace had her own theory. "You're both right. They're clouds and then rain and then clouds again. But God makes all that stuff happen."

"I think clouds go on forever," said JJ. "Watch them move. They go away and we can't see them anymore. But somebody else can see them. People on the other side of the world can see them."

"My mom says that's what happens when we die," Hannah informed them. "She said just when they are leaving us, they are arriving somewhere else. And when we are crying, the people who are greeting them are happy and cheering and laughing."

For a while, they silently watched the cloud parade. Sometimes a cloud would brazenly block the sun, but the old sun always shooed it away and came back to warm the grassy hill and the children lying on it. JJ sat up and asked, "Do you think that's how it will be if my deddy has to go to jail?"

In all the madness of the past year, JJ had not discussed this possibility with his cousins, nor they with him. Silence bookended his question.

After a moment, Patience spoke up. "My mom and dad said that is a big person problem."

"I think what they meant," offered Hannah soothingly, "was that it's for grownups to handle and figure out what to do. We don't have to do that. But if....if Uncle Bird has to go to jail, then it is our problem. Especially for JJ."

"So if we're not supposed to do anything," Anna Grace began, but faded off for a moment. "JJ, what did Uncle Bird and Aunt Steph tell you? Did they talk about what might happen?"

By now, all the kids were sitting up. JJ hugged his knees and rested his chin before speaking. "They told me that Deddy will come home. We don't know when, but he will come home. He will. And until then, I can still see him and talk to him; just not every day. Other than that, everything will be the same. I'll go to school and Mr. Moose will visit and at Christmas time..."

JJ buried his face behind his knees and began to sob. He had been courageous enough to stand up to bullies and strong enough to help keep up his daddy's spirits, and dedicated enough to get good grades - even in math - but he sensed a change in the air recently that filled him with a profound grief. This was adult sorrow and he had no filter and no point of reference for it. This was sorrow beyond tears, but the tears came anyway, swelling his throat and wracking his slim frame. And perhaps the fact that the girls did not weep - not one of them - was indicative of how they too had been tempered by the events of the past year. Instead of weeping, they drew near their cousin and held him, letting him know wordlessly that, for now at least, he was safe.

When the tears had turned to snuffles, JJ wiped his nose on his shirt and stared into the distance. When someone finally spoke, it was Hannah: "Hey, we forgot something!"

The hopeful tone in Hannah's voice compelled Anna Grace to eagerly question what it was that they had forgotten.

"We're the Mustard Seed Kids," Hannah continued, "and we haven't even thought about that in a while. They say this is a big person's problem and not ours. But when we pray, we let God handle it, no matter whose problem it is. And nothing's too big for Him."

"We haven't had our prayer circle in so long," Anna Grace asserted, "and I don't know why! Remember the Bible tells us that when two or more are gathered together in His name, He is with us."

"I have faith as small as a mustard seed," piped up Patience.

Hannah quickly agreed and Anna Grace stated, "I have at least that much faith! And together we have even more."

After a long moment, JJ spoke. "We didn't know what to do when Hannah was lost. But God took care of us. I don't know what to do now."

One by one, they stood on the hillside, lifted their arms to the middle of their little circle, and joined hands.

Hannah: "Our Heavenly Father, we come to You because You always help us when we are lost. And You always find us. Thank you, Lord, for bringing us out of the dark."

Anna Grace: "When Hannah was a lost lamb, You brought her home. And when JJ and Patience were deep in the well, You brought them home. And we thank You."

Patience: "Thank You God, for letting us be your lambs. And for being our Shepherd."

JJ: "Thank You, Lord, for bringing us all out of the forest when we were lost, for leading us to Thumper, for protecting us and helping. Thank you for bringing my deddy home some day, and for showing us what to do until then. Thank you for taking care of us...until you bring us all home...in the Sweet By and By."

Jackie hollered out the back door, "Y'all come in, now. It looks like rain." They had hardly noticed the dimming of the sun. Looking up, their fluffy white clouds had all gone to heaven and been returned as slate gray storm clouds. They walked back to the house in silence.

This was, indeed, one of those childhood days that they would always remember. That Saturday at Gommi's, the next day with church and rain, and the first day of the trial, would forever be vividly imprinted on the minds of these four, who called themselves The Mustard Seed Kids.

By dawn, the steps and lawn of the courthouse were already seething with bodies. Groups shouted at other groups, banners were held and signs waved. Reporters and photographers grabbed and grasped at anyone attempting to enter or exit the courthouse. Deputies scurried to usher several well-dressed people into the courthouse and chaos erupted.

Before their car even approached the courthouse square, Jackie could see the madness. She leaned out of the open window, searching for a parking space. Abruptly there was a burst of movement toward their vehicle as they were recognized. Larry gunned the SUV, pulled into oncoming traffic, skirted the sidewalk for the remainder of the block and disappeared behind the building.

At that same moment, Jason and Stephanie were attempting to cross the courthouse lawn. News reporters spotted them and charged in their direction. Shouts burst from the crowd, as those carrying signs began to yell phrases of support or derision, and cameramen attempted to catch any potential dirt for the nightly news. Two deputies rushed to Jason and Steph and managed to usher them into a nearby doorway, blocking the entrance behind them. As one, reporters pivoted hungrily toward their cameras and began to share the latest and most sensational development with their viewers.

At that very instant, local reporter Deaundria Keana Kelly appeared on the Veitch's television screen. Behind her could be seen handsome newsman Chance Mitchum speaking into his station's camera, and behind him, reporters as far as the eye could see. Kelly's voice was almost swallowed up by the throng around her, but she managed to make her point about this, "...vicious and unprovoked murder that has shattered this community." Fights began to break out and the camera was jostled and shaken. Jennifer, Hannah, and Anna Grace watched the TV screen in speechless horror.

Hours later, after the reporters and activists had their fill and fed their needs, a few stragglers made their exit from the empty courtroom. The lawn was strewn with city workers cleaning up the mounds of debris, and the entire scene had an exhausted feel to it. Larry could be seen helping a fragile Jackie into their car. Jim was close behind. Jason and Stephanie were making their exit through a door near the back dumpsters. Jason and Jim made eye contact and halted. For a long moment, they stood, just looking at one another across a distance of only a few feet. Stephanie watched until she noticed two deputies eyeing them narrowly. Gently and reluctantly, she urged her husband into a waiting car. Jim turned and was making his way to the parking garage, when he noticed a familiar figure sitting on the courthouse steps. He walked over and hunkered down beside Moose. In a bit, Jim addressed the big man, "I know Jason appreciates you coming to court every day. If they'd let him talk to us, he'd tell you that."

"I wanna help," was Moose's only response.

"You are helping. Just by being here."

"Naw. I *wanna* help. But I can't help him. He's stronger than me."

"He needs you, though. He needs us all."

Moose turned and gave Jim a bruised look. "I couldn't do that."

"Couldn't do what?"

"What he's doing. Hearing them say all those things about him, and he just sits there. I can't hardly stand it. I wanna git up and shut 'em up for good."

"Oh, yeah. I know that feeling."

"But he can take it. He's stronger than me."

"You know where that strength comes from, don't you, Moose?"

"Yeah. Maybe. No."

"When we don't have the strength we need, we let God take over. He likes that. He tells us in the Bible that His strength is made perfect in our weakness. Isn't that wonderful? We just do our best and let God do the rest."

"How do you let go, Mr. Jim?! I don't know how to let anybody do anything for me. Gotta do it by myself. How do you let go?"

"Well, that's a tough question. God wants us to do for ourselves. But sometimes he lets it be all too tough for us, just so we'll remember that He is really in charge and He can do all things. So we let go. It takes faith, though."

"What if you don't have enough faith?"

Jim shifted his legs and laughed. "Oh, it's not about having enough faith, it's just about having some faith; the tiniest bit of faith. There's another passage that says, *If you have faith as small as—*"*

Moose joined in and they recited together, — *"as a mustard seed, ye shall say unto this mountain, Remove hence to yonder place and it shall remove..."* *

---

* **KJV Matthew 17:20**
* **KJV Matthew 17:20**

Jim added, *"Nothing will be impossible for you."***

Moose repeated, *"Nothing will be impossible..."****

A little breeze kicked up and touched the early spring grass. The two lone men sat in the late day shadow of the formidable building that towered behind them.

Jim leaned back on his elbows and inhaled easily. "Just a little faith. The faith of a child. Sometimes I think the little ones have it all over on us when it comes to faith. They haven't been taught yet that faith has limitations. JJ and the girls believe with a purity and strength that amazes me daily. We call them The Mustard Seed Kids."

"I gotta kid," Moose offered. "Little boy, but I can't get to him."

"Maybe you can get to him. Maybe faith can get you there."

"I wanna have faith like Jason and them kids. I wanna do something that shows the world I'm strong, but inside strong. And I don't wanna hurt nobody no more. I wanna be strong. Like Jason. Like the kids."

"Me too, Moose. Me too."

Morning. Fingers of sunlight reached through the kitchen blinds. Jackie was seated at the bar, a stack of documents and papers before her. She was dressed for another day in court and gazing intently at the files. Behind her, Larry tended to the coffee and straightened his tie in the reflection of the coffee maker. He poured a mug of coffee and placed it beside Jackie, still lost in her papers. Then he turned and poured a mug for himself. As he passed by the bar, Larry moved the untouched mug closer to Jackie and closed her fingers around it. Without breaking her gaze, she lifted the coffee and blew and sipped.

The Veitch family now marched through their morning routine with the silent precision of a drill team. As Jim rose from the table, Hannah removed his plate. Anna Grace brought a paper sack lunch to her dad, as Patience lifted his coffee cup and returned it to the sink. Jennifer straightened the handkerchief in her husband's pocket. All

---

** **KJV Matthew 17:20**
*** **KJV Matthew 17:20**

movement stopped. One by one, Jim kissed all his girls and silently left the house. His four girls watched until he was gone.

Jason closed Steph's car door for her and crossed in front of the vehicle, dropping into the driver's seat, as he had done so many mornings. But this morning was different. He shut his door and put on his seatbelt but did not start the engine. A moment passed and then JJ spoke, "Deddy."

"Yes, JJ."

"I'll be late for school."

"Yes, JJ."

Still the engine did not crank and Jason did not move.

"Deddy?"

"Yes, JJ."

"Don't be scared of the court today. We been praying for rainbows."

The engine cranked up and the car pulled out of the drive and disappeared down the street.

Jennifer had a queasy feeling in the pit of her stomach as she drove to pick up JJ after school. The feeling of dread had been building since the trial ended and the jury went into deliberation. With a murder trial, the jury could be out for days, weeks. Michael Kam had told the family that they should hope for a long deliberation; a short one almost always meant bad news. But waiting was soul-killing. It had been a long and wearying climb for the entire family and they had often wished for an end to it. Now that they were looking at an end (when? today? six months from now?) it felt as if they were standing on a precipice, overlooking a gaping chasm. Jennifer almost longed for those days of waiting for the trial to begin. She slowed for a squirrel. As she sped up again, she reflected on the savage television coverage they had watched earlier. Why didn't she turn it off as soon as it came on?! How could she let the girls see it? Glancing in the rear view, she looked at her daughters who were sitting quietly in the back seat; so well-behaved today. And she thought of JJ and Jason and Stephanie. And the sick feeling crept back in.

The day was overcast, but Jennifer parked under a big shade tree anyway. Silently exiting the car, she leaned in the window and looked at the girls. "Y'all wait here; JJ's class will be out in a couple of minutes." And she began to trudge up the brick sidewalks that sliced the little campus into grassy islands. It was amazing: As she looked about at the lush spring growth, it suddenly struck her that one year ago today, they had looked at spring with such hope, believing this would all be over in just a few days. And now...how many springs might they have to —

Jennifer shook away these dark thoughts and picked up her stride. Heading to the big stone stairs in front of the building, she retrieved her cell phone and checked it for the millionth time.

The school gardener paused in his tasks at exactly the right moment to witness an alarming scene. Across the campus, he observed a woman who abruptly stopped, one foot on the sidewalk and one foot on the stone steps. She appeared to stare at her phone for a long minute and when it dropped from her hand, she didn't pick it up. Then she began to sway precariously, her knees giving way. Dropping his spade, he dashed toward her, but in a blink she had disappeared through the big front doors.

Jennifer ran down the hallway, her low heels pounding out echoes on the shiny floor. An elderly teacher glared sternly at her. Her purse swung wildly and then dropped, scattering its contents with a clatter. She didn't break her stride.

The classroom door was flung open so powerfully that it hit the wall with a bang that caused Miss Inez and her entire class to jump. Jennifer spit her words out in a rush. "It's in — the verdict is in — JJ's daddy — they've reached a verdict."

Judge S. Carroll was such a small woman. Jackie had thought at one point, irrationally, that maybe they could be friends and if they could just talk woman-to-woman she could make the judge understand. But even if she could convince this powerful woman, the judge only read the paper that the jurors gave her. Judge Carroll addressed the packed, silent courtroom, "Ladies and Gentlemen, let me remind you that this is a matter that requires utmost dignity. As I said before, a young man has perished and another's life is in the balance. There will be no cause for outward disagreement or celebration no matter what the verdict is. Has the jury reached a verdict?"

"We have, Your Honor."

"Please hand the verdict form to the bailiff."

The juror handed the verdict to the bailiff. The bailiff handed it to the officer. The officer ascended the steps to the judge's seat and handed it to her. She lay it flat on her desk and opened it. And read. Then she looked up.

Stephanie's daddy was cradling her like a child. Larry was holding Jackie but she was only aware of a buzzing in her head and in her body. She could hear what was being said, but couldn't understand it. The jury had only been out for one day; she tried to remember if Kam had told them a short deliberation was a good thing or a bad thing. The judge ordered Jason to stand. He did so, with Ellis on one side and Kam on the other. Stephanie felt a sudden urge to reach forward and grab Jason and run. He was only inches away, just in front of her! She could reach him before anyone could stop her. But her body didn't move.

The school room was a still photograph, capturing a moment when lives are forever changed. Miss Inez broke the stillness and burst into motion. She grabbed as many little hands as she could and swept from the room, commanding over her shoulder, "Come with me."

Jason's head jerked back abruptly and his knees buckled. Before he could fall, Ellis and Kam grabbed him, one arm each, and held him up. Then Judge Carroll began to read, "The State of Georgia versus Jason Richard Veitch. We, the jury, find the Defendant —"

Miss Inez charged down the long hallway, pulling and trailing students. Jennifer, now with the girls in tow, clattered behind them. The same stern teacher glared at them with her best shame face, but it had no power over them. They all poured into a massive doorway. Over the door was a simple plaque: CHAPEL. Once inside, Miss Inez began, "I know that each and every person in this room has prayed that JJ's daddy would be returned to his family. And all the big, smart people told us it would not happen. But we believed, didn't we? We asked and were faithful and patient and now we have received. He's coming home to stay. Let's say thanks, okay? Before JJ leaves to celebrate with his family, let's just have a quiet moment of thanks. Who would like to start?"

JJ's tiny figure broke out and moved to the center of the crowd. For a moment he hesitated and appeared to be overwhelmed. Hannah moved out and took his hand. Then Anna Grace and then Patience joined him. They connected their hands, forming a perfect and complete circle. The Mustard Seed Kids were back. Silently, all the little children came forward, growing and expanding the circle. Sunlight streamed through the chapel's stained glass windows, casting a rainbow of color upon them.

Outside, on the courtroom lawn, the usual spectacle had completely changed in tone. The reporters and cameras were still there, but the sense of urgency surging through the crowds had vanished. Groups broke off into smaller groups. People smiled for the first time in a long time. Standing for a moment at the top of the courtroom steps, Jason and Jennifer looked down at the lawn and the crowd. Jason spotted Jackie and Larry, surrounded by well-wishers. It occurred to him that he had not been allowed to hug his mom in a long, long time. Stephanie, seeing the look in his eyes, gently nudged him toward his parents. The steps were easy. Moving through the crowd was easy. Everything would to be easy now. When Jason spotted Jackie, the urge to rush into her arms faded. They just looked at one another, both knowing that there was a lifetime of hugging ahead. Easy; no rush. Jackie held out her hand and placed a folded piece of paper in Jason's hand. Jason stared at it a long moment before reaching into his coat and placing a folded paper in his mom's hand. They smiled. And they hugged. And suddenly JJ surprised his daddy by appearing out of the crowd. He leapt upon Jason, and was clinging to him like a little monkey. JJ wasn't going to let go; nobody could make him. And as Jennifer and Jim and Stephanie moved close, Hannah and Anna Grace and Patience, overwhelmed by the pure joy of the moment, jumped Jason as well. They all tumbled to the ground and out of nowhere, one more family member was greeting Jason on the courthouse lawn: Thumper was licking his face, with a slobbery smile. The family laughed easily. Flat on his back in the grass and covered by Mustard Seed Kids, Jason looked up. The clouds had lifted completely. It was a beautiful day.

Chapter Twelve

After

One year later, on a softly warm and beautiful day, a single flatbed train car sat on the railroad tracks. The grassy acres surrounding it were dotted with brightly colored stands, tables and booths, food, banners, and balloons. Big folks were dressed in light, colorful outfits and their kids flitted and drifted about like butterflies in the sunlight. Many of the children wore t-shirts which proclaimed *I Am A Mustard Seed Kid*. A raised platform, festooned with bunting and lined with chairs, held a podium and a microphone. Music serenaded from big speakers and mixed with shouts and laughter.

Stephanie stood under a big willow, talking with a man who had a dark, stern face. Suddenly he burst into laughter and his entire demeanor changed. He had been one of the jurors for Jason's trial. He sat on the front of the jury box; in fact he finally revealed himself to be the foreman and delivered the very piece of paper which proclaimed Jason innocent. He often stared at Jackie with his hard, dark eyes, and she feared him most of all. His stern face and long gazes convinced

Jackie that he wanted to take Jason down. But in fact, he was only overwhelmed with the entire tragic situation. He was looking for the truth, and once he heard it, he championed Jason's release. Stephanie had also feared him and expected the worst. On the day of the innocent verdict, Steph had spotted this foreboding juror on the courthouse lawn. More than anyone on the jury, she wanted to thank him, and ask his forgiveness for judging him. When these two strangers met, they fell into each other's arms; awash with tears and gratitude and release of emotion. But today there were no tears. This was a day for celebration. And the stern-looking man and Stephanie laughed like old friends.

The year that had passed since that day on the courthouse lawn brought many changes. It had not occurred to the Carpenters and the Veitch family that most of the people here today at this gathering by the train tracks were not known to them before Jason's incarceration and trial. Yes, Fontella and her husband were out on the grassy lawn, as was Ellis and his wife. But there were also jurors, and there was Moose, and people who had been silently supporting the family and praying for them. JJ's teacher and classmates joined him on this day. And chatting easily with Jim was a certain Mr. Vertue — but that's another story.

Looking distinctly out of place in a suit and tie, a tall distinguished man mounted the platform and nodded at those seated there. He gestured for the music to be lowered, and when he had the attention of most of the crowd, he began to speak.

"Good day, everyone, and thank you for joining us. My name is Stanley Bannister and I am here as representative of the Guinness Book of World Records. Today we will witness an attempt to do something that has never been done in the history of mankind. I am here to document that event, should it actually occur. Behind me you see a train car, weighing approximately twenty-five tons. And today, a man unaided by anything other than his own muscles, will attempt to pull it along these tracks. Please help me welcome to the stage, Mr. Louis Dunivan."

Moose, wearing a track suit and with his head bobbing awkwardly, took to the stage. Mr. Bannister handed him the microphone. Moose attempted to speak, faltered, and went silent. He lowered the microphone and closed his eyes for a bit, then gazed upon the crowd. There, the loving faces of Jason, Jackie, JJ and so many of his friends gazed back. A thin little boy standing near the front began to clap his hands. The crowd erupted into applause and Moose smiled sheepishly. Moose raised the microphone and began to speak.

"I forgot what I was supposed to say. But that's alright, I reckon. I do want y'all to know one thing, though. This Mr. Bannister says I won't have nothin' to help me but my muscles. That's not true. I learned a lot over the past year. And one thing I learned come from the Bible. It says, *I can do all things through Christ.* * So if I do anything here today, it's because I have faith. I only have a little faith — just about the size of a mustard seed — but I believe that's enough. I — I believe. And too, I got love. I got the love of my friends and the love of my little boy out there."

Moose pointed at the skinny kid who had started the applause and he sent his dad a huge, snaggle-tooth grin. "And I got the love of my new family. And the bravest man I ever met. Mr. Jason Veitch taught me that love is stronger than muscles. And he's my friend. So...I...and that's all I got."

Moose ducked his head and strode from the platform to warm applause. He walked directly to the train car's coupling. Mr. Bannister and several officials drew near, followed closely by the crowd and photographers and reporters. Moose removed his track suit top to reveal a *I'm A Mustard Seed Kid* t-shirt. Then he sat upon the tracks, hands poised above the coupling. For a moment he just stared at the train car. Then he rose, but only to his knees. This huge man bowed his head and clasped his hands as humbly as he had seen JJ do. After a moment, Moose lifted his head, rose to a standing position and walked over to his little boy. He lifted him up into his arms and said to his friends and family, "They tell me I can't do this. It's true. I can't. But God can. And if he wants it to move from here...to there...then it will."

Moose approached the flatbed and placed his boy on it. He gestured to JJ, who dashed forward, and was lifted onto it. Little children,

---

* **KJV Phillippians 4:13**

wearing their Mustard Seed shirts, were lifted onto the train car by the adults. The car was alive and heavy with children, laughing and waving to their families. Moose quickly positioned himself at the front of the train car, sat down, grabbed the coupling with both hands and braced his feet against the ties. Silence. Muscles began to lock and blood vessels to stand out on the big man's body, as his face turned a deep red. He pulled and strained. Nothing happened. He pulled again. Still nothing. He pulled again. Then suddenly, with a trembling jolt, the train car began to move. Then it moved a little more. And more and then faster. Moose walked himself backwards, pulling with all his might, as the crowd exploded and cheered; little children jumped and danced and clapped. Mr. Bannister completely lost his cool composure and was dancing as well, as the cameramen and reporters recorded the momentous event. The Veitch family and the Carpenter family and all their extended family had much to celebrate on that bright Georgia day.

JJ glanced over at Wyatt and at Tucker (who was known to the family as The Little Mooseling) and Hannah, Anna Grace, and Pay-Pay as the car moved slowly down the track. All up and down the car, he saw friends. All across the grassy expanse he saw family. He looked at Moose and marveled that such a powerful man could admit that faith is stronger than muscles. He thought over all the lessons that he and his family and Moose had learned; lessons about strength and endurance and bullies and faith and each other and themselves. And he and many others were learning to turn down the noise and listen: Ask, then listen. These were only vague and fleeting thoughts in the little boy's head and he surely would not have been able to put them into words. Yet. What he did know was that, with faith the size of a mustard seed, mountains will indeed move from here....to there....

ALSO BY MICHAEL MCCLENDON

THE BIG BOOK OF MONOLOGUES
A MOUNTAIN TOO HIGH
CRITTER

Made in the USA
Monee, IL
14 November 2023

46528946R00080